Arlo and Jake Enlist

Book One of the Adventures of Arlo and Jake

By

Gary Alan Henson

A Magnus Somnium Publication

Dallas, Texas

Copyright © 2012 by Gary Alan Henson

Revision 2 October 2017

All rights reserved. No part of this publication may be reproduced electronically, mechanically, by photocopy, recording, or any other method except for brief quotations in reviews, without the prior permission of the copyright owner. This is a work of fiction. References to names, characters, places and incidents either are the product of the author's imagination or are used fictitiously, and any resemblance to any actual persons, living or dead, events or locales is entirely coincidental.

Acknowledgements

I would like to thank my wife, Debbie and my daughter Amber for putting up with yet another session of silly ideas and puns. Your moral support and many suggestions make this so much better. Love you.

I'd also like to thank Rocky Angelucci for editing support and the super book cover.

Books by Gary Alan Henson

Science Fiction
'Arlo and Jake Enlist' (2013)
'Arlo and Jake Galactic Boot Camp' (2014)
'Arlo and Jake Lost Partner' (2015)

Ghost Stories and Paranormal
'Genome' (2006)
'Etchings' (2015)
'Walk with Me' (2016)

Chapter One

Damn, I have got to remember to close that shade at night.

The bright morning sun is frying my retinas right through my sleep-gummed eyelids. Last night's hot wings and beer slosh around dangerously in my gut as I roll over to escape the solar onslaught. *Hmm, give it a minute; I'm sure it'll settle again.* I try not to move, waiting for the rumbling to subside. *Ahh, that's better. I think we're good.*

And then the volcano stirs in my gut, sending out deep, warning bass burbles. *OK, time to sit up and see how this day is going to start.* Gathering my awesome inner strength, I carefully scoot to the edge of the bed and push myself up to a sitting position. My legs hang over the side of the bed, feet firmly planted on the cool wooden floor.

Made it. I let out a long, slow sigh of relief. Then the rumbles crescendo for a moment. *Damn, going to be that kind of morning, is it?* Then abruptly it stops, and I feel the pressure ease. *Uh, oh.* I feel a big old burble wave traveling up my stomach, then my chest and finally pushing out my throat. "Buurpphhppttt." *Ahhhhhh, that's definitely better. At least I won't explode now.*

The fermented wing sauce geyser is gone but the taste is, well, gross. Funny how chicken wings taste great the first time but not so good the second time. I wait another moment to make sure Mount Vesuvius has settled back down then push off the bed. *Hey, look at me, I'm upright again! Whoo Hoo!* Well, it's time to get another day of freedom and swell times started.

As I gingerly stretch my arms up, I'm greeted with the normal snap, crackle and pops of my body of 65 years. *Atta boy, you manly structure of studliness talk to me; remind me I'm alive.* It takes me a few more stretches before the bones settle back into their sockets and stop their complaining.

"Ok. Time to make some java and get my heart started," I say to no one in particular. Good thing, too, as I'm the only one in the house. Well, except for Arlo, wherever he's hiding. He's probably already had his breakfast out on the porch. Arlo strolls to his own tiny little drumbeat.

I get my morning scratch session in as I mosey into the little kitchen down the hall. I'm not a slob, but I can see that the dirty dish pile is getting a little out of hand. *Ok, today I get this room cleaned up.* I look around at the small kitchen. *Well, maybe later.*

Above the stove, the clock hand continues its endless arc behind the clear glass; 1 o'clock. *Hmm. I'm up a little early today.* Well, no problem. I push some dishes around and fire up the stove. Time for some bacon and eggs to go with my coffee.

Fifteen minutes later I'm savoring over-easy eggs with Tabasco sauce, crispy mesquite smoked bacon, some pulpy orange juice and coffee. I take my coffee blonde and sweet, just like my women. Right. That was a great quote when Deedee laughed at it with me. She always laughed at my jokes, no matter how many times she heard them. I take a sip and raise my cup out the window view towards the beach. *I miss you babe. God, how I miss you.*

I set my cup down and gaze out the window, listening to the waves and soft wind through the beach grass surrounding my little cottage. There are a few locals combing the sand and laughing. Three years. It's been three years since cancer took my Deedee. It feels like yesterday. *Ok, enough.* Time to get my busy day started. I am retired after all; time to enjoy the fruits of my labors.

The shower is weak and tepid. *Gotta call the plumber and get the hot water heater fixed.* I step out of the shower and towel off quickly. I never look in the mirror anymore; I know my gut is winning the fight for dominance. Why rub my face in it? Still, it feels damn good to be alive. I think.

I throw on my usual shorts and Hawaiian shirt and grab my favorite cap on the way out the front screen door. The small porch faces the beachfront 20 yards away. A nice breeze is flowing in from the water, keeping the temp down for now.

The little cottage in Port Aransas became my home shortly after Deedee died. We found it years ago on a spur of the moment trip south from our home in Lewisville, near Dallas. We loved to come down during the summer with a box of books and some Texas Red wines. Then we would spend weeks enjoying the simple life. Life was good. Very good.

So. Where the hell did Arlo get to, and where is my beer cooler?

***

"I'm telling you, Arlo, retirement is the greatest invention since the root beer float," I murmur, stroking Arlo's snout ridge absently. Gazing out at the gentle waves from the porch, I scooch my butt around in the old wooden lounge chair, trying to get more comfortable. The cushions blew away in the last squall. Who needs 'em? My backside is cushy enough.

Sighing as I find that sweet spot on the chair, I glance down at the big, emerald-green panther chameleon perched on the flat chair arm. Arlo has stretched out his body to its full foot and a half to soak up the hot afternoon sun. He's chosen a lovely mottled sea-green for his morning camouflage.

"Thirty years twiddling bits as a software programmer was enough, little buddy. It was time to stop making the corporate fat bosses fatter and live the good life. Wadda ya say, bucko?"

Glancing over the top of my Fat Tire bottle, I wait for a reply from my little cold-natured friend; sort of. After half a dozen bottles of my favorite brew, I tend to forget Arlo is only talking back to me in my imagination. I think. I hope.

Right on cue, he turns his freaky little left eye 180 degrees to look back at me, keeping the right one glued forward. A tiny little Sean Connery voice echoes in my head. "Sure, Dude. You coded like a lion, man. Now you deserve to kick back and watch the hotties strut down the beach. Live it up dude, for tomorrow you die." His eye flicks forward again. *You're creeping me out, little buddy. Yesterday you sounded like James Dean. Pick an imaginary voice, and stick with it, will you? Hmmm. One more brew and it's time to lay off for the afternoon.*

I take another swig and straighten out my favorite Hawaiian shirt: bright green parrots in a jungle scene. It matches my lime green beach shorts perfectly. I settle back and look up to the beach just in time to catch a pair of beach bunnies strolling by in the latest swimsuit fashion; flesh colored, almost invisible thong bikinis. *Nice. I'm not sure if it's fashion or just a creative way to use knitted dental floss, but my complements to the designer. Sigh. Too bad I have grandkids older than these two.*

Settling my Navy ball cap down a little further on my head, I tip the bottle at the redhead. Usually the girls passing by just ignore me and my old fashion displays of gratitude, but this time she actually smiles, gives me a wink and a little wave as they walk by.

My heart pops up into my throat for a moment. *Now what the hell would you do if they come over and start talking to you? Iron-willed you are not, and all you'll remember afterwards is the lack of tan lines. Will you remember the color of their eyes? Hmmm, I'm sure they have eyes but... nope, got no clue.*

Arlo actually moves his tail a micro meter, startling me with this rare demonstration of effort. "Wow, Arlo! You need to rest after your morning exercise?" Arlo whips the left eye back at me for two seconds in disdain. Then I swear he grunts. Lizards can grunt, right?

I realize my social faux pas immediately. "Sorry, man. It's the sun. I'm suffering from dehydration, I swear." His eye bobs up and down a couple of times and then whips forward again to scan the beach.

"Sheesh, a little touchy are we? Not enough gnats for you this morning? Man you should be in gnat heaven today; they're thick as flies…" *Hmm that was funnier in my head I guess.*

Peering down the neck of the dark brown bottle tells me a sad tale: empty. I drop it into the box next to my chair with its brothers. Reaching over Arlo, I pop the lid on the cooler and snag another cold, wet bottle.

The emergency church key is on a string attached to the back of the chair, ever at the ready. I grab it and flip the cap. *Ha! Number 7 and got it on the first try!*

Tossing the cap into the box, I chug half the ice-cold nectar in one draw. It burns the back of my throat on the way down. A wonderful, brain freezing kind of burn. *Ahhh, life is good.*

I settle the bottle on the chair arm and sit back. *I should get up and take a pee before I fall asleep... or I could enjoy the buzz and the warm breeze first. Hmmm, decisions, decisions.*

*****

A white hot poker is being jammed through my ankle. My leg seems wrapped in electrified barbed razor wire as I jerk awake, screaming like a 500-pound pig in heat. I try to grab my leg, but the touch of my hands feels like burning coals with six inch spikes.

Falling back into the chair, I wait for the stroke that has to be coming next. I'm shaking violently; my heart is racing and pounding in my chest. I'm really trying to get my scream down to choir boy level, shutting my eyes tightly trying to concentrate on not dying.

Forcing myself to relax and calm my breathing, I can finally feel my heart rate drop below 200. The SPF2000 is mixing with my tears, stinging like mustard sauce. Wiping the goo away, I try to open them again. Slowly, my eyes focus again, and I can see three pairs of shapely legs in the sand standing at the end of my chair. *What the hell?*

I manage to bite my lip and silence the embarrassing squeal. Lifting my hat slowly, I wonder if this is still part of some demented dream. Nope, the legs are connected to three of the most voluptuous, gorgeous examples of the female form I have ever seen. Way hotter than the dental floss twins earlier today.

They're lined up like the final three in a beauty pageant. On the left is a pony-tailed Blond Bombshell; five foot two with eyes of brilliant blue, her bright yellow beach wrap barely concealing her body. The Goddess stands in the middle of the trio in a bright green one piece bikini. She has flaming red hair, green eyes and fire engine red lips. Then there's calendar girl, Miss March, straining a stark white fishnet bikini to its limit. Her dark brunette hair is cascading down her creamy shoulders and flowing down the front of her suit. If this is a pain induced hallucination, don't give me any medicine! Even the best of my dreams don't conjure up beauties like this!

Then the Goddess taps my ankle with the tip of her umbrella. Fresh waves of agony flash up my leg. *I can bite my tongue off now or let loose with another sissy boy scream. So* scream it is! They can probably hear me scream 40 miles away in Corpus Christi. I can imagine the retired couple under their beach umbrella sucking on pina coladas hearing my wailings. "Listen, Edith, they've found another closet Democrat. Poor thing."

"Stop crucifying my foot, you exquisite goddess! Stop, pleasesese!" The last word is drawn out and sort of bubbly and weak. The Goddess raises a perfectly sculpted eyebrow and withdraws her stick of torture. She flips it up and opens it to shade her perfect, flowing red hair.

That's when I notice her eyes. Well, I try to notice her eyes. I try, I really do, but getting past the rest of her tanned perfection is taking every ounce of energy I have left.

Her voice snaps my attention past her throat and lips and finally into those incredible emerald green eyes. "Espi plorkum, nute atoony mazeka? Shasha nesta coop, noshertock!"

Uh what? I tap the hearing aid in my left ear a couple of times. It's been picking up the local Tex-Mex station lately. It buzzes a little but that's all. I try to shrug my shoulders at The Goddess and wince as my skin explodes in fresh pain.

Blonde Bombshell on her right nudges The Goddess and points to her dangling earring. *Ok. What's that about?* The Goddess looks irritated but tries to discreetly reach up to her ear. She twists the earring, coughs and lowers her hand.

Again she forms those perfect lips, but this time I hear, "Crucify? Are we interviewing a wus?" She turns to the blonde and raises an eyebrow. Blonde Bombshell nods her ponytailed head slightly and steps back a bit. The Goddess slowly turns back to me lowering her eyebrow, a small smile forming on her… [***Author's Note: Ok, ok so from now on you'll get it, right? Perfect bods, perfect hair, eyes you can fall into, blah, blah, blah. You've got an imagination, use it. Trust me you won't even be close, but we're wasting time here.]** "Are you in pain? All I did was tap your foot," she purrs.

Still shaking with pain, I manage to look down at my leg. Funny, it wasn't beet red and swollen when I got that last beer. Ah. I look up at the sun's position. I've been asleep for at least four hours. Thinking back on the other times I have cooked my skin, I figure this time it's going to take a trip to the ER, with at least a month in rehab. With any luck no skin grafts. Nice.

"Oog, ahga, icka," is all I can manage as the pain level continues to rise. I wait for my sausage of a leg to explode, spewing cooked Jake Jasper all over the beach. All I can do is point to the pulsing red balloon and babble.

The Goddess tilts her head, eyeing my leg. She turns to Miss March to her left and says, "Surgeon, can you do anything for this blubbering fool's extremity, or should we just puncture it and put him out of his misery?"

Kind of a strange name isn't it? 'Surgeon'? Miss March steps up next to The Goddess and raises her hand up to her finely pointed chin. "It would be a simple matter, Capt... err my lady. Shall I administer a, ah, healing potion?" She's holding a small silver disc in her palm. *Potion? From a fancy compact?*

The Goddess looks down at my leg and sighs. "Yes, ah, lady Nanel, let's get him healthy again. He's of no use to me in this condition."

Lady Nanel? Whatever. "Surgeon, doc, whatever you are, help me, please!" is all I can squeak out.

Miss March steps up to my leg, and I recoil. Unfortunately for me, my leg does not come with me since it's stuck to the chair like a bratwurst to a grill. There goes my heart rate again. I'd scream, but I've lost track of where my lungs are.

She passes the little disc a few inches above my leg, from foot to hip and back again. Its surface pulses with rainbow colors and little sparkles of bright blue and green. The disc emits some muffled little 'bloops' and 'bleeps' and 'bloorps' as she stops back at the foot. She presses the middle of the disc and a small needle extrudes from the edge, right above my big toe. *Oh, now, you are NOT...* She slowly tilts her head up, giving me a titillating view of her magnificent uh, assets. *My god, how does she stay upright?* Just as I realize why she is distracting me, she plunges the needle under the nail of my poor puffed up toe.

I draw in my breath to scream my lungs inside out, right in her beautiful face, when I notice there is no pain. She stands abruptly, giving me a full view of the toe and my leg. It's like someone is squeezing a long red balloon that's leaking air. The color is turning from that hellish crimson to a nice light brown. It travels up my leg and my side and then down the other side to the toe on my other leg. I feel a very strange 'tingling' under my shorts and have a brief moment of panic. I hastily glance up at

Lady Nanel's clinging bikini top and feel mini-me swell with pride. *Whew. I'll check on you later, dude.*

In seconds my blistered, cancerous body is tan and 'normal' again. Normal for me is 40 pounds of extra buttered bread and beer, but hey I'm certainly not complaining. And the pain is gone. My skin actually feels 'good'. You know, not stretched and dry. I am marveling at the transformation when I hear, "Hello. Hello. Mr. Jasper?"

I'm grinning from ear to ear as I turn my gaze back to my saviors. I feel amazing! And standing in front of me are three gorgeous women looking expectantly at me. *OK. What am I missing here? Think, Jake, think. This is one of those 'once in a lifetime' moments. I just know it!* And... nothing. I haven't a clue what to do next. I'm representing my gender at my typical awesome level. Lots of dud and no stud. Sigh.

Finally, The Goddess rolls her eyes and turns to Ms. Bombshell on her right. They have a whispered, one-sided conversation. Ms. Bombshell nods her ponytail several times and shakes it once or twice. I lose count as I gawk at her perfect face moving back and forth.

I glance back to Lady Nanel. She lifts a slender index finger to her pouty lips and gives her head a small shake, then quickly drops her hand. *OK, what the hell was that about?* I'm about to ask when The Goddess says, "Enough. We'll deal with this after we're on board again."

She turns back to me, clasps her hands daintily in front of shapely hips, gives me a talking-to-a-little-school-boy look and says, "Mr. Jasper, we're here to offer you employment of the most exciting kind. It's a chance for a life that few men have the balls, I mean steel, to accept, but all wish they had. Are you up for more excitement than you have experienced in your entire, pathetic short life, far flung travel, exotic ports of call power and wealth and all that it can buy?" She unclasps her hands and slowly moves them around to her back, accentuating her figure, she caps off the move with a drop-dead smile.

"Huh, I guess." *Again. Dud. What the hell? I know my testosterone is low but damn, what is wrong with me?* I look back and forth between the titillating trio, trying to form a coherent thought. I look around at the beach, my beach house and down at Arlo. Arlo? "Hey, where the hell is Arlo?" I turn in my chair, start to get up to find my little lizard buddy when I spot him next to the beer cooler in the sand. His color is near perfect, but I've gotten pretty good at spotting him. It's kind of a game we, or rather I, play. Arlo stands still somewhere, and I look for him. It's more fun for me, I guess.

"Hey, there you are buddy. Where are you going? I need you here to guard my back against these Amazonian beach women." As I lean down to pick him up, I hear a loud crackle sound, like a bug zapper frying a fat June bug. The sand has a very weird look, sort of like stars in a black sky. *That's odd.*

Chapter Two

"Hmmm. Thath fells gud, kept dobing thath. Oooww! Hey, stup ith! Geth haway frum dere you morron, thath's pribate and thensitive!" *Wait, why does my voice sound like I've got a mouth full of jello? Where the hell am I?* There's plenty of light, but everything is out of focus. I'm trying to focus my eyes, but it's like peering through clear foam, not thick but light with billions of tiny bubbles floating up. *Whose aquarium did I wake up in?*

Aquarium. *Holy crap, how am I breathing under water?* Instinctively I shut my mouth to hold my breath, panic rising from my belly. I try swimming up, but I'm not getting anywhere. I'm stuck to the floor. Wait, not stuck; I can jump up, but I drop back down without floating at all! All I'm doing is flailing around in a big pool of sparkling fizz. I'm gonna drown in soda pop. How humiliating.

Wait a minute; I was fine a moment ago. What the hell? I force myself to relax and try to take a breath of the foaming bubbles. It's like sucking in humid air around Houston-warm and moist. *Hell, I can breathe this stuff fine!* Damn, it feels good too; my lungs suck it in eagerly. Every time I breathe in I can feel that warm tingle you get from the first sip of a dirty martini out on the patio. *Nice. Definitely not soda pop then.*

I can move around, -sort of. At least I'm upright in this super-sized Jacuzzi. I turn slowly in a circle trying to figure out what I've been dipped in. It feels really good whatever it is. It's pulsing all around me like someone stuck a speaker in it and they're playing some ZZ Top- a deep thrumming vibration I can feel through my whole body.

There's light pouring in all around me, through the gel, making the bubbles sparkle like tiny diamonds. *OK, let's go see where the light's coming from.* I push forward into the goo but only get about two feet when I smash into a clear wall with my nose. Crackle, buzz *Ouch!* Whatever it is it tries to push my nose back into my face with a little static burn thrown in. *That's just rude, folks.*

More cautiously this time I try peering through the wall. I can see a little more clearly than before but everything is still distorted. Whoa, there must have been a sale on white enamel paint somewhere. And funky colored lights. And people dressed in blue and white uniforms of some kind.

A blurry silhouette strolls past my field of view. *Wait; is that a pair of gold epaulets? What the hell? Oh wait, I get it now; I'm having another sunburn-induced dream, that's it! Whew. For a minute there I was worried.* Walking around inside a giant lava lamp sucking on warm soda fizz has got to be a dream. A nice, weird dream, but I get those sometimes. I think it's the tequila.

"PLEASE STAND AWAY FROM THE FIELD, SIR." A deep, resonating baritone voice pipes in on my right, and I jump back a step. OK, so it's not a dream. I think. I ooze my way over to the source of the voice and try to peer past the wall. An elfin face, hovering down at the four-foot-ten level and framed in a white hood, thrusts up to the other side of the wall; the bright pink lips move. "I SAID STAND AWAY FROM THE FIELD, SIR. NOW!" I jerk backwards another foot as the deep voice booms from a cute pixie mouth. *That's going to rate some time with a therapist. Geesh!*

The gel vibrates with the voice again. "STAND BY FOR SPECIMEN RETRIEVAL. MR. JASPER, PLEASE STAND PERFECTLY STLL. THANK YOU." I think the voice is Pixie Girl. Before I can ask, small holes appear in the floor and the bubbling foam that surrounds me is being sucked down. Not drained, or allowed to flow, or slowly decant, sucked down like a thick milkshake in a big straw. The fluid is stripping my skin like 100 grit sandpaper. Damn, that hurts! It's all I can do to stay upright.

Finally, the foam is completely drained, and I stagger a little. Shaking myself, I start to open my mouth to complain; I do that a lot. I'm hit with a hot, pink, vinegary liquid spraying from all around the tube. Not a nice gentle shower spray, no; it's like they're firing alcohol from a pressure washer. *Damn!*

Suddenly the blasting stops. The liquid drips off me as it's sucked down the holes. When it finally stops, I'm glistening, burning and raw. "Damn it, you jackasses, that bloody hurt! What do you think..." A tornado of hot air blasts me from all directions, and I hear, "Stand still, sir. Please, stand still!" The voice is definitely female now and more than a little threatening, so I try to man-up and remain still against the blast. What's left of my skin feels like its being stripped off my body.

Abruptly the maelstrom stops. Keeping my eyes closed and my hands in front of my face, I do what any manly man would do; I whine. "What, no sandblasting treatment? Why don't you just throw me in a blender with a few pounds of steel wool and some alcohol?" I wait a few seconds for the alcohol, but when nothing else happens, I open my eyes and lower my hands down to cover my jewels. I notice my nakedness sometime during the tornado treatment.

I hear "snap, crackle, snoop-bloop" as the 'field' disappears around me. Pixie Girl walks towards me holding out a green robe and sandals. Her hood and suit have been replaced with a bright white suit jacket and pleated white skirt that hugs her hips. She's incredibly cute with short bobbed, bright pink hair and brilliant blue eyes. "Please dress and follow me, sir." She waits patiently while I stare around me.

I'm in a large circular lab of some kind. The walls are lined with consoles, large display screens and flashing colored lights. A dozen or so techie-looking types are manning the keyboards and switches. All of them have turned in their chairs to look at my outburst. The techies are women of all sizes, shapes and colors; all of them would stop a Navy Seal in his tracks.

To my left is a video screen that stretches from floor to ceiling and occupies a quarter of the curved outer wall space. It's showing some space opera movie, complete with hokey space ships and explosions. For some reason I'm drawn towards the screen. *I gotta get one of these for my den.* Suddenly the screen flashes a brilliant white and the floor trembles. Miss Pixie is suddenly at my side. She says with some irritation, "Perhaps you could robe yourself now, Mr. Jasper, so that I might return to my battle station? It's really most important, I assure you."

I grab the robe and hold it in front of me, gazing around the room. Usually in my dreams everyone ignores me when I'm naked and walking around. My body is lean and trim and my vision is clear as well. That's how I know it's a dream. Not this time. Most of the lovely lady techs are watching me openly; some look like they are enjoying my discomfort a little too much.

Trying to ignore them, I slip on the robe and shoes and then look up at Pixie. "I'm sorry. This dream is really amazing. Beautiful women, a space lab that would make Spielberg drool. And that movie you're showing is awesome."

That adorable little pixie face looks up at me for a moment, smiles, and then she slaps me so hard I drop back onto my butt. Bending down to my level, her voice is as cold as an Eskimos' nose. "I hope that convinces you that this is not a dream, sir. We don't have time for this nonsense. Pull yourself together, or I'll have security bind you and drag you along. Make up your mind right now." Her left index finger is poised over a small tattoo on her right wrist. When I don't respond she says, "This is a com-tat for Security. Shall I press it, sir?" The 'sir' is more than a little strained.

The truth is seeping into my freshly scrubbed brain. *This is real. All of it.* Pixie sighs, but before she can call the cops, I grab her arm. "Wait. I'm sorry. If this isn't a dream, my world just got pulled inside out. What would you do if this happened to you?" I say more harshly than I intended.

She looks at her arm, raises a petite, arched eyebrow and turns back to me. I immediately let her arm go. Gazing at me and then out to the battle scene, her face softens a bit. "I'd probably be bloody bonkers by now, sir." Stepping to the side, she motions me up and forward. "Please. Let me get you to your station, and I'll explain what I can on the way. It's the best I can do for now."

We start towards the wall opposite the screen. The room is ignoring us now; everyone seems intent on whatever people do in these labs across the universe. "Thank you, Miss?" I'm struggling to keep up with her, but I need a name. I'm old and decrepit, but I'm polite. "What do I call you?"

Miss Pixie presses a different tattoo on her wrist, and a small section of wall disappears in front of us just as we get there. "Try Lieutenant Tillet for now, sir. I'll tell you more when, and if you are cleared to know it."

Outside the lab, the Lieutenant steps onto a white floor tile and points to a tile to her right. "Stand here, please." I move forward to the spot just as the tile starts pulsing red. Immediately some kind of invisible field grabs my feet. "I can't move my feet, Pixie, uh, I mean, Lieutenant Tillet." I struggle for a moment and then look at the Lieutenant.

She's smiling at me with her arms crossed. "Pixie? Relax and enjoy the ride, Mr. Jasper." She presses another tattoo spot, and I notice for the first time that her hands, wrists and upper arms are covered with interlacing tattoos, just visible on her skin. The one she just pressed turns bright red. "Don't fight the transport tile, Mr. Jasper. We need to go."

With that, she presses another tattoo. I can feel my tile rise a few inches from the deck. Something is holding my lower body solidly to the tile as it starts forward, just behind the Lieutenant's tile. *This is awesome*! Lieutenant Pixie looks back as the tiles start to gain momentum and winks at me. "You may want to close your eyes, sir. The first time on a transport can be a little, uh, disorienting." She turns back 'forward' and clasps her hands behind her back. She's leaning forward like a magnificent sixteenth century wooden ship figurehead ... only with pink hair of course.

I'm about to protest her lack of faith in my studliness when I notice that we're no longer inches off the deck. We're whizzing towards the center of a huge space at least 20 feet off the deck. It feels like we're moving at Mach Two, but there's no wind. I feel like I'm part of the pulsing frisbee under my feet. Showing my escort just how under control I am, I yell "Holy Crapppp!" It sounded more intelligent in my head.

Lieutenant Pixie's tile shifts to the right and back to match its speed with mine. She turns slightly to her left and grins. "No need to shout, sir. The transport has a field that surrounds us and allows for communication." She looks forward and then back to me. "We're about to transit through the ship's axis tube towards the bridge. Take a deep breath and let it out, sir. We're almost there." She enjoys this a little too much, me thinks.

Before I can protest, the tiles tilt 'up' into a tube that spans at least a dozen football fields across. The tiles and my feet are gliding 'above' the shaft surface, and my head is pointing towards the center of the yawning gap. After an involuntary yelp, I settle again and look around the tube. Now I know how astronauts feel as they move around in space without gravity. My frame of reference keeps changing, and it's all I can do to keep my stomach from doing the jitterbug.

We're passing ring after ring of insanely busy compartments and landings and things beyond my imagination. There are tiles flying everywhere, manned with men, women and other things that pass too quickly for me to identify. Crap, some of these can't be living things; they've got flailing tentacles and tools attached to long metallic arms. That one looks like someone welded all the left over parts from the last space opera together and added a big eye on top.

Looking 'down', I almost lose it. I have to close my eyes and wait for my brain to stop vibrating. Only a few seconds pass before I risk another peek. We must be much closer to the 'top' than the 'bottom'. This shaft looks like its miles 'deep'! Without something to measure it against, I'm at a loss, and that's where my vertigo is coming from.

I turn back to 'up'. "Is it much further, Lieutenant?" I ask hopefully. I can see a bright spot growing at the end of the tube. And it's growing larger very quickly.

"That is our destination as you've already observed, Mr. Jasper." Lieutenant Pixie is pointing at the bright circle ahead. "Please stand still until I tell you to exit the transport, sir."

Seconds later the tiles rotate again, and we're whizzing away from the tube axis and into what must be the bridge. The tiles slide to a stop at the edge of a large circular room completely domed in those video screens. The space is huge, encircling us with gleaming white surfaces, blue and green console screens and red chairs.

Every station is manned with beings intent on their stations. Some are standing, others seated, some moving swiftly between stations. It's a controlled chaos that brings back memories of the control room on every submarine I ever served on. Everyone is focused on their job and yet also aware of everyone and everything around them.

My 'transport' square has turned white again and I gingerly test my footing. *Great, now I can run away. But to where?*

Lieutenant Pixie marches up to me like a miniature tin soldier and takes my elbow. "Stand up straight, Recruit. The Captain will only have a moment for you. She's rather busy right now." With that she drops her hand and turns to stand beside me, all proper and at attention. *Crap. I've been here before in another life. I've been written up for Captain's Mast on more than one submarine. I'm on board a friggin' spaceship for 10 minutes, and I'm already going to stand in front of the Captain to explain myself? This must be a new personal record.* I grin to myself to cover my nerves.

Lieutenant Pixie must have seen the grin because her voice is like ice as she whispers, "You're at attention, Mr. Jasper. I know you have the background to know what that means." The silly smile instantly vanishes from my face. In its place is a neutral, attentive rigidness I haven't felt in decades. "Better, sir.

The next few minutes may determine if you're allowed to become a recruit or just another slacker we throw back into the bucket."

An officer turns towards us from the center of the bridge. I can sense the Lieutenant stiffening further, and I try to stand taller as I watch a woman in an impossibly white and gold uniform step quickly towards us. *Crap!* It's The Goddess from the beach.

If anything, the uniform accentuates her luscious form more than the bikini, but her face is pure ice. Her flaming red hair is back in a bun with four, 12 inch golden needles sticking up from the bundle. She has a short golden staff held in her right hand and tucked back under her arm. *Uh, Captain?*

Just as she stops in front of us, Lieutenant Pixie snaps a salute and holds it. "Lieutenant Tillet and Recruit Jasper reporting as requested. Sir!" The Lieutenant's eyes never waver from some invisible dot directly in front of her.

Captain Goddess turns her head to my escort. "At ease Lieutenant. I have only a few minutes for this interview. What is your impression of this recruit?"

I finally come to my senses and blurt out, "Recruit? What recruit? I've been kidnapped, and you know it because you kidnapped me. What the hell is going on here?" The shock of the vat of fizzy mucus, the flying tiles and seeing The Goddess on the bridge of this huge bucket of white enamel finally hit me, and not in a good way. I feel anger and fear prickling up and down my spine.

Captain Goddess snaps her head towards me and freezes my rant before I can gear up again. "Silence, Mr. Jasper." From nowhere there appear four huge men in brilliant red uniforms with some sort of red and gold staffs pointed at me.

At a hand motion from The Goddess, they step back in unison. "That's not necessary, Marines, please stand down." The red suits step back two more paces, but I can tell from their looks that I'm 'this' close to having my head ripped from my scrawny neck and shoved into a deep, dark hole.

The Goddess, I mean, Captain Goddess, looks me in the eyes. This time her voice has just a bit of sympathy in it. "I understand your confusion, Mr. Jasper. And I apologize for calling you to the bridge rather than meeting you in the Medical

Section. But circumstances have forced me to remain on the Con. We may have to engage the enemy at any moment."

Her face softens some more and I can see a faint smile now. "I wanted to give you the full tour myself, Mr. Jasper. Ordinarily I would have time to show you Triumph, give you the reasons and history that forced me to pluck you and your partner, Arlo I believe, from your comfortable beach."

She nods to Arlo and says, "Arlo, I apologize to you as well of course. Your life will be much different if you and Mr. Jasper decide to join our cause. And you deserve to be treated better than I have been able, but as I said circumstances have forced me to be occupied on the bridge."

Arlo shifts on my shoulder and bounces a little. *What the hell, little buddy? She must think you're some kind of talking pet.*

Before I can explain about Arlo, she turns back to me and says, "I hope there will be time later for me to properly interview you, Mr. Jasper. For now let's begin the interview and see how far we get. Can you hold your questions for a few minutes Mr. Jasper?"

Ok. How do you say 'No' to a beautiful woman in uniform? Especially one with a squad of red suited jar heads pointing nasty looking staffs thingies things at you!

"OK. I'm listening, for now."

"Thank you, Mr. Jasper. I promise you will not regret it." She gestures around the bridge and says, "At the highest level this is the battle ship 'Triumph'. She is a Nova class vessel, manned by a crew of over 10,000. We are currently pursuing an enemy that is engaged in exterminating terrestrial species on all the inhabited planets they encounter." Her face clouds and she continues softly, "As in all wars, there are casualties. Recent conflicts have cost the Triumph dearly and the crew's complement has suffered."

The cloud passes as she fixes me with blazing green eyes. There is steel there now, hard and angry. "I need my ship at full strength, Mr. Jasper. To do that I need to recruit replacements for the brave crew who gave their lives to defend planets like yours. Can you…" At that moment the loudest klaxon alarm I've ever heard started pulsing from everywhere inside the bridge. The Captain spins towards the bridge deck where chaos has just erupted.

At the same time it hits me. *Did she say 'replacements' and 'crew who gave their lives' in the same sentence"? Crap, this is NOT good and NOT going to happen*!

"Lieutenant Tillet, escort Mr. Jasper to the crews' quarters, and return to your battle station immediately. Dismissed."

She abruptly turns back to the bridge, and I suddenly realize what this is all about. *They've conscripted me, for God's sake. I've been 'pressed' into service in some bloody galactic space armada!* "Like hell, I'm dismissed! You can't just come down and kidnap me for your damn space fleet! Take us home, damn you!"

I step forward to grab the Captain and talk some sense into her. I don't make it a single step before the world goes black. *Ah, for crap's sake, not again…*

Chapter Three

How did that elephant herd get inside my head? One of them stomps on my eyeballs when I try to raise my head and the world explodes into glassy shards. *Ouch!* Trying not to move again I use my spidey senses to tell I'm locked into a pillow of some kind of hospital bed. *Yeah, right.*

Every muscle in my body feels like lead. I can't move anything. Trying to open my eyes brings a low groan from the effort. *OK, one more time.* I try to pry my lids apart again and look around. This time it's more of a grunt than a groan, but at least I get a response from someone.

"Please don't try to move, Recruit. I'm the ship's surgeon, Lieutenant Commander Nanel. You're being restrained until I hear from the Captain's aide, Lieutenant Tillet." I can sense someone approaching to my left. I try again to open my eyes, and this time I succeed. "Well," she says, "you seem determined to hurt yourself, Recruit. Admirable effort but you should conserve your energy."

I continue to wheeze and grunt, trying to focus on the voice. Damn, it's the brunette from the beach, dressed in brilliant white and gazing down at me with a sympathetic smile. "All right, Mr. Jasper. I don't want you damaged further. I'll release your head restraint. But I warn you, you need to keep still and let the meditable work on you."

She's a vision from a submariner's dream. Soft brown hair is flowing around her shoulders and across her spotless, white tunic. Her back is ramrod straight holding her frame perfectly with the curving waist and bold hips. She has that hourglass figure men only fantasize about. The pleated skirt is the perfect length to show Cyd Charisse gams. *Damn and hot damn!*

She stands and again goes to the head of the table. I hear a soft 'beep' and instantly the weight lifts from my face and head. I blink a few times and slowly look around. All I can see behind her flowing skirt are more of those long polished white benches with displays and blinking lights.

I try my voice: "Where am I? What happened?" I sound like a frog on crack, but I want to know, so I swallow and try again. "I was on the bridge talking to The Goddess, and suddenly the lights went out. Again."

Walking back into my view, Lieutenant Commander Nanel smirks and says, "The Goddess?" Her face lights up in understanding. "Ah. You mean Captain Starla, I believe. Yes. 'The Goddess' does fit her nicely." She touches a tattoo on her arm and asks, "How is our patient doing?"

I hear a disembodied voice reply, "The damage was minimal, sir. I've repaired the breaks and contusions. There will be some bruising for the rest of the day but no permanent damage. I can release him from stasis now if he refrains from exertion for the next two hours."

"Do so, Ship." I feel the rest of the lead-suit-feeling fall away and can't help letting out a thankful sigh. When I try to sit up, she puts a cool hand on my chest and says, "Not quite yet, Mr. Jasper. Give yourself a few minutes before you attempt to rise. Ship has been repairing your body, and it will take a little longer for you to be fully in control again."

"Repairing? What did I break?" This sounds bad.

She puts a cool hand on my leg. My heart rate skips from 'stressed' to 'insane' in less than a second when she gently squeezes it. "I believe you attempted to touch the Captain. In full view of her marine guard as I understand it. Most impetuous and dangerous, I must say. It's only because of your recent rejuv that you're not back in the tanks." I can't tell by her slight smile if she's impressed or amused.

"You mean those jar-hea… I mean, marines knocked me out without touching me?" Thinking back on the moment I made the connection. "Ah. Those long sticks. They zapped me with those overgrown toothpicks, right?"

"They're called kanntums, which means 'Spirit Staff', Mr. Jasper. I assure you that you felt only a minuscule portion of their power. It was enough to shatter several bones and render you unconscious. The rejuv nanites provided some protection and are now helping repair the damage." She turns to the console, looking at something and turning back. "Your internal functions are quickly returning to normal. You also no longer need your hearing device or eye glasses."

Looking into those gorgeous eyes is melting my stress quickly. I reach up to my ear, and sure enough, no lump of plastic, but I can hear just fine. Looking around the room and back at the beautiful woman standing next to me, I realize it's all in focus. Sharp, clear focus. I haven't seen this clearly in decades. *My god, I can see the flecks of gold in her incredibly blue eyes.*

Wait. "Nanites? You mean those little molecular robots the egg-heads keep claiming we'll have in only a few more years? You guys have them? How do they work? How did you introduce them into my body? Will they always be in there, or do they dissolve or get flushed out? How do you…"

"Please, Mr. Jasper. All in good time. For now just the easy answers." She sits down on the table next to me, the curve of her skirt hinting at the marvelous leg it is hiding. She lays her hand on my chest, and this time the cool touch is calming.

"The nanites were introduced into your body when you first came on board and were placed in the rejuv tank. It's standard procedure, both for your protection and for ours. You could carry any number of annoying or even deadly infections."

"I don't remember any shots, ma'am, just swimming around in that bubbly goop."

"That goop is a rejuv mixture of bio-genetic complexes and nanites. Both are engineered to enter every orifice in your body and repair and modify your cellular structure."

"Every orifice?" This sounds just a little yucky.

"Yes, Mr. Jasper. Shall I tell you how the rejuv enters…"

"Wait, wait. No, I think I'll pass on that for now, ma'am." *Sheesh.* She nods and removes her hand.

She looks up above my head. "You have a visitor, Mr. Jasper. I believe you'll want to discuss your mutual situations while you rest. I'll be back soon. Do not try to exit sick bay, Mr. Jasper. Ship will not allow it."

Without further explanation, she stands and walks towards a blank section in the wall without stopping. It looks like she's going to face plant into the wall, but it cycles her through barely in time. An opening in the wall just seems to appear in front of her, and after she steps through the wall, is back. No 'swooshing' two sided panels, no weird irising circles, nothing. The door just appears and then poof, it's gone. *Ok, I won't ask how the ship could stop me for now. Maybe later.*

I look around, but I don't see anyone else in my view. I start to rise, but my body is not cooperating yet, so I just lie back. "Ok. She said I had a visitor. Who are you? Could you maybe move so I can see you?" I wait for some movement, a face, a body, tentacles, anything.

Then I notice a tiny green claw tapping my left shoulder and turn my head slowly to the left. Arlo is squatting just above my left shoulder on the edge of the bed. His right eye is focused on me, and his claw stops tapping. "Hello, Bucko," echoes in my mind in full blown Scottish drawl. "Are you done slacking off, mate?"

I smack my knee on the side of the bed trying to jump off, and then once again I'm on my ass on the floor. Staring up at the edge of the bed, I can see Arlo's little head peek down. My jaw drops open as I hear, "Close your mouth, Rube, you're embarrassing me."

Arlo shifts a little and crouches down on the bedside looking down at me with those beady little yellow eyes. "Beady yellow eyes? I'll have you know my eyes are brilliant cadmium, and I'm quite proud of them." Arlo's eyes do a slow roll while his voice rattles around in my head. Then he snaps both of them to focus on me. "Oh. And by the way, we have a telepathic link now, just in case you've missed the obvious."

Since his scaly little mouth hasn't moved, and since I have to assume I'm not dreaming, I close my mouth and slowly stand. "Uh, ok." A profound leap of faith occurs, and all I can say is "OK." And that's how the human mind deals with the absurd and the sublime.

Somehow I know it's true. Arlo and I have some kind of link and wait... a mind link is one thing but Arlo is not... And then I hear the voice again. "Oh yes, Big Guy. Actually, I am sentient," the voice rolls into my mind. "Not only that, but there's a good chance I can burn you in an IQ test, at least in some areas. Take that, Hairy Butt!" The last word is punctuated with a whip-snap of his little green tail.

    I drop into a chair by the bed and wait for the world around me to stop tilting. My mind is drifting in circles, not really thinking about anything in particular; just listening to the buzzing questions in the back recesses of my noggin.

    All around me are gleaming white consoles with soft blue and green mosaic touch pads and muted blue screens with strange symbols and letters scrolling or blinking across them. There are no sharp corners; everything's all rounded and molded contours as though the designers didn't believe in 90 degree angles. Every surface flows into its neighbor seamlessly as though it's all one composite piece. It reminds me of those pictures of the human brain with its folds, one upon the next, never ending, and all part of the same entity.

    "As I understand it so far, Bucko, that's pretty close to the facts." Arlo's voice is soft in my head, like he's trying not to scare me. "The ship was designed by its own Artificial Intelligence. I think that everything around us is built to accommodate many different species of life but can also be controlled by the ship." Arlo walks slowly along the bed towards me then stops and squats down again. "I'm sure we'll find out more when we can talk to Ship again."

    "Talk to Ship? You mean like 'Computer, locate Ensign Red Shirt'?" I shift around in the chair looking at the walls and panels. "Computer. Where the hell am I?" I shout. Silence. Nada. Nuttin'. Spinning the chair around to face Arlo, I raise my hands questioningly. "Looks like the computer is taking a nano break. I didn't hear anything, did you?" I look around at the room again. "Maybe this really is a wacky dream. That's it. I'm really in the hospital with a morphine drip while they figure out what to do with my organs. I can see the headlines now. 'Local stud muffin forgets his sun block and cooks in his own juices. Funeral attended by thousands of distraught beach bunnies.'"

Arlo whips his tail once, and I can see his eyes rotating around. "No. You're not on the donor table, Jake. And I really am talking to you. If you think you're confused, stop and think about this from my perspective. This really is the first day of the rest of my life, Dude."

That catches me off guard. "Great. My pet lizard is now spouting John Denver song lyrics. I'm almost afraid to say this, but could this get any weirder?" I cringe and look around the spotless lab waiting for a crack in space or for something slimy with big eyes and wearing a fish helmet to appear. When nothing reaches out to eat my face, I turn back to Arlo. He's tapping his claw again.

"Are you done freaking out on me, Jake? I could use a little pet-to-master interaction here." He emphasizes the 'master' word a little too sarcastically to be an accident. "Do you get it yet? This really is a first day for me, you hairy bag of pus. Before today, I was a handsome, happy young creature of the wild. Warm sun, juicy bugs and hiding from you was a great day for me. Now I've got all this crap running around in my head. Bye, bye simple life of joy. Hello crusty old conscience and silly morals. What demented being decided to add right and wrong to your frantic philosophies?" The whole time Arlo's ranting he's rocking back and forth on one front and the opposite back leg, his eyes rotating asynchronously like demented little yellow balls. Sorry, cadmium yellow. He stops rocking and locks both eyes on me.

"Uh?" Am I a Renaissance man or what? I sit back and drop my hands in my lap. "Look, Arlo, this is just a wee bit wacky for me too. Forgive me for not adjusting faster but jumpin' Jupiter on a stick, WHAT THE HELL do you want from me? I'm locked in some kind of Frankenstein's lab for germaphobes in a FRIGGIN' SPACE SHIP!" I throw my hands up and wave them around the room. "Do you SEE where we are buddy?"

Then it hit me. Buddy? "Oh. Right. And let's not forget I'm talking to my little green lizard buddy. Hmm. Ok, Arlo, give me a second." I sink back in the chair, look at Arlo as a 'he' instead of an 'it' and then let my brain turn to soup for a moment.

Arlo actually shakes his little head back and forth a couple of times, both eyes lasering the ceiling and then me. I can sense his frustration at me as he concedes, "Ok. Fine. Let's just let your old noggin' percolate a couple of minutes while this ship is in the middle of a shoot-out in space. Nothing to worry about in this scenario, right?"

I look at Arlo and then at the 'screens' with the wild fireworks that are lighting up space all around us. "Oh my God, Arlo. This is real." I glance back at the bed and see Arlo walking back up to the head of the bed, facing the screens with me.

"Yeah. Bloody grand, isn't it?" I swear there's a grin on his scaly little face. Before I can retort, the wall behind me melts and in strides Nanel. "Please return to the bed, Mr. Jasper. It's time you and Ship get to know each other."

Chapter Four

Nanel's uniform has some disturbing stains and marks on the front, ruining the sparkling white material. The front lapel is unbuttoned and hangs loosely, showing just a hint of her marvelous cleavage behind an almost sheer blazing red blouse.

She motions to the bed and says, "Please lie down, Mr. Jasper. This will only take a moment, and a moment is all I can spare right now." She presses a small tattoo on her arm and then turns to a console behind her. The panel seems to come to life as her fingers fly across it. "Ship, please extract a sample from Mr. Jasper's cortex and prepare an implant."

I have started towards the bed automatically, my Navy training from years ago kicking back in at the sound of her voice. Submarine. Spaceship. Hey, they're both big tin cans with people inside and bad stuff outside, right? And ten years of following a command structure does tend to affect the way you think and act.

However, I stop at the word 'cortex' and stand back up next to the bed. "Excuse me, ma'am, did you just say 'cortex' and 'extract' in the same sentence?" My fight verses flight reflexes are definitely primed for flight.

Raising my right hand, I start counting out my issues on my fingers, one at a time. "I just found out my pet is telepathic and sentient; that I'm onboard a spaceship that is by the way, in the middle of a stellar shootout, and that the three gorgeous women I met on the beach are actually officers in some friggin' Space Navy. Oh, and let's not forget that I've been conscripted into said friggin' Navy."

I cross my arms defiantly. "Before any implanting is allowed in the hollow space between my ears, I'm going to need a little more information. Is that really too much to ask?"

Nanel slowly turns from the panel and faces me; her face is stern but sympathetic. She seems to contemplate smacking me upside the head, but instead her eyes soften. She motions to the bed and then sits in the chair next to it. "Please sit Mr. Jasper. I could have you restrained, and this would be over in less than a minute.

The process is reversible and poses no harm to you at all, however I believe in this case you deserve some answers first. But I must be brief, Recruit. As you have noticed, there is a battle on and I'm needed elsewhere."

The tone of her voice is enough to keep me quiet as I sit on the bed. Arlo walks up to the top of the bed and squats, obviously wanting answers as well. I hear him sort of whisper in my head, "This should be good. Nice of you to finally stand our ground, Testiclese." I shoot Arlo a 'Shut up, Twerp' look and turn back to Nanel.

Those deep, stunning eyes are focused squarely on mine as she gives me the short and sweet. "You are being recruited as an ABS, an Able Bodied Spaceman, in the service of the FTG, the Federation of the Thirteen Galaxies. We represent and protect trillions of sentient beings in a vast area of this universe. We are at war with the Galactic Houses of Aquinoxous, the GHA."

Her face turns to stone when she continues. "The GHA is composed of beings that require a liquid environment to survive, usually water. Their colonization program is expansive and devastating. When the GHA finds a suitable planet to colonize, they use planetary engineering to aquaform that planet, without warning, without regard to any existing life. They consider terra life forms the same way you might consider insects or vermin."

I look out the view screens at the flashes and explosions, wondering just how far away those little blinks of light really are and who or what is being vaporized behind the flashes. "Are we in a battle with this GHA now?" is all I can manage.

"Yes, Mr. Jasper, we are. We've been skirmishing with this battle group for months, sometimes the victor and sometimes not." As if the universe is listening in on our little conversation a deep rumbling sound is accompanied by a tremor I can feel through the deck. Nanel gazes at the view screen and back to me. "Currently we are not. I need to finish, so please remain silent." She reaches back to the panel and presses a button then turns back to me.

"Your planet, Earth, is one of the planets the GHA will eventually discover and aquaform if we fail. It could happen in your lifetime, Mr. Jasper. You have been recruited to replace crewmen who have fallen in this and other battles. We need your mind as well as your body to help man this battleship or we could fail and your Earth will become another colony for the GHA. If we lose, every soul on your planet will perish." Her voice turns grave as she leans forward. "I need you to join our crew, Mr. Jasper. Will you help us? If so, I need to start the process, to see if you are physically and mentally qualified for service. I need to do it now."

You would think I would demand more. Or jump up and slam into the wall where she entered, hoping a door would appear. Or maybe start screaming like a banshee. Instead, I sense somehow she's telling the truth. *Earth turned into a swimming pool for a bunch of soggy monsters? I don't think so!*

I turn to Arlo and cock an eyebrow. "Well, little buddy, what do you think? We can go back to the beach and lay around 'til they finally dump my dry-roasted body into a hole or we could join up and kick some squidish butt. Just so you know, I'll leaning towards the butt kickin' option."

Arlo does that head jerk back and forth thing a couple of time and I swear he shrugs his little shoulders. "Dude, she had me at Able Bodied Spaceman. I hope we get spiffy uniforms!" He fixes his freaky eye on me and says, "Steaming cow pies dude, of course yes, what are you waiting for, cowboy?"

I can't keep the smile off my face as set my jaw and lay back on the bed. "I believe you had another appointment, ma'am, uh sir. We're wasting time."

A flash of surprise lights her eyes, then a brief smile. "Perhaps we were right after all, Mr. Jasper. I am most impressed." She presses something on the panel. "Ship, please proceed with the implant. You may restrain Mr. Jasper until he has recovered, then release him. Contact me when he is able to proceed."

"As you wish, sir." The disembodied voice chimes. The bed starts to lower.

Lieutenant Commander Nanel rises from her chair and starts for the door, or wall or whatever it is. A warm mist of something that smells like waffles sprays around my face. As I start to fall into a sweet sleep I hear her say, "Welcome aboard, Recruit. May the gods watch over us all."

A wonderful euphoria is spreading throughout my body. *Hmm, this is sooo good.* I drag my eyes back open and see a big green, scaly nose looking down from the top of the bed. One of Arlo's eyes zeroes in on my silly face, the other is watching something to my right. I hear a soft whining sound from that direction. "Oohh, you do NOT want to know what they're about to jam into your brain box, Dude."

Chapter Five

"Wakey, wakey Jake. Ship says it's time to rise and shine." I can feel a tiny claw tapping on my brow and hear that Scottish drawl in my head. Weird. Now he sounds like John Wayne trying to do an impression of Sean Connery. *Make up your mind little buddy.* "Ship says Nanel will be here in two minutes. We have to be ready to leave sick bay. So hit the deck, me Matey, Arrrggghhhh." I swear there is a little pink patch on Arlo's eye as the haze starts to clear. For crying out loud he's created the patch on his skin, complete with a little line around his head. "How do you like the eye patch, matey?"

"Nice touch, Arlo. I didn't know you had that kind of control. But you might want to make it black instead of pink, you know, a little more macho." Arlo shakes his head a little and the patch turns glossy black.

"That better, bucko? Sheesh, everyone's a critic. Now, get your butt outta that rack, Jake."

"OK, fine, I'm up already." I feel around my head for patches or bandages. Nada. Not even a suture that I can feel. *That's odd, I don't heal all that fast.* Sitting up, the room spins just a little, and I grab the edge of the bed. "Whoa, that was some good anesthetic or whatever they sprayed me with. Gimme a second to find my feet."

A soft female voice resonates in my head, "Please stay on the bed for a moment, Mr. Jasper. I need to run a few interface tests."

I spin around looking for the source of the voice, then the conversation with Nanel replays in my head. *Oh yeah, something about an interface to the ship.* "Umm. So are you the ship's Artificial Intelligence? How the hell am I supposed to keep all the new voices in my head straight?" I look over at Arlo for some sympathy.

"Please remain quiet, sir, this will only take a moment. You are about to receive a small history lesson through your interface."

I start to protest, because when you're told to remain quiet that's what every smart ass does. Instead I freeze; my eyes wide open as I watch a wacked-out 3D movie flash by in my mind at hyper-super-duper speed. It's like I'm watching a thousand Discovery Channel episodes all at once. But somehow I completely understand everything that's going past.

I'm whizzing through history and science and biology. *What in God's name is that tentacly thing that just ate some poor guy in a spacesuit?* Now I'm looking down at a planet from space that looks like Earth, only it's mostly land instead of mostly water. All around me, dozens of huge red and green ships that look like they're made of some kind of bizarre coral pop out of nowhere. The ships start shooting brilliant rainbow colored beams at the planet from all sides. I zoom in to the planet's surface through the blinding rays and stop at a hundred feet or so above the surface.

Incredibly weird buildings are literally melting and flowing into the ground, which is also melting and morphing into some kind of bubbling, smoking mush. Then I see the 'people'. They look like those little troll dolls the kids used to play with. They have squat green and purple bodies with wildly colored hair flowing above large green eyes. Oh my God, they're melting and bubbling. Just like the buildings and the ground. I can't hear the screams but their mouths are contorted and wide. Then they're gone, flowing down into the horrible, frothing soup.

Suddenly I'm back on the bed and the lab snaps back into focus. "Damn." It's all I can think of. "Damn and double damn."

I look around the lab and find Arlo. "Damn, buddy, did you see that?" Arlo favors me with a nod.

"Yeah, I saw it. That's pretty much what I thought too, Jake. That dog won't hunt."

The soft voice continues in my head, "The lesson is complete Mr. Jasper. You need to assign me a moniker so that we can link quickly. You can use the word 'Ship' if you like, but a unique name is easier for most new recruits to grasp."

Good. I need something to get the images of those freaky little people melting and smoking into the goo out of my head. I think about it for a moment, trying to find something that relates if that's possible. Then it comes to me. "PIP. I'll call you PIP."

The voice isn't in my head this time but seems to emanate from all around me. "As you wish Mr. Jasper, but I find no reference to that word except for a musical group from your planet. May I ask why this moniker?"

"Sure. One of the last projects I tried to get funded was for an advanced computer interface to control a biogenetics lab. My team was making great progress before the funding was cut. PIP stands for Protocol Interface Program. We had a rudimentary holographic avatar, voice interaction and a pretty damn sweet personality module functional. I believed enough in it to apply for patents for the concept with my own money."

"PIP it is, sir. You need only think or say that name, and we can communicate. I'll be monitoring you at all times through your interface. I do not normally engage in conversation unless addressed by a moniker or if I ascertain from context that you require my attention. Is that clear?"

"Yeah, I've got it PIP."

At that moment, the wall melts and Lieutenant Commander Nanel steps through. She's dressed in some kind of casual uniform this time. It's an almost sheer dark blue blouse with some sort of medical emblem above the left pocket and a pair of black pants that leave just the right amount to the imagination. Her hair is tied in the back with a simple, long red ribbon. I remember the battle stains and glance back at the screens. No flash, no explosions. Nothing but stars, and I think some of those are other ships.

"Is the battle over, sir? How long have I been out? Can…" She raises her hands to stop my questions.

"One thing first before we proceed, Mr. Jasper. Yes the battle was won, though just. How do you feel?" She steps beside me and starts to examine me from head to toe. That's when I notice I'm naked as a jay bird. I notice something else also. I feel different. Refreshed and energized. It's like I just chugged a dozen espressos with a cup of sugar. I can't stop the grin from spreading across my face.

"I see you're starting to notice the effects of the rejuv procedure. Please relax and remain calm. I'll explain." She moves to face me, examining every part of my face with her long, delicate fingers. Her face is set with that determined concentration you see in surgeons around the Universe who care about their patient.

"You should be noticing that your body has been undergoing some changes due to the rejuvenation process. The gel you were immersed in and some procedures performed while you were in the healing tank have been tagging your DNA to approximately age 25 in Earth years. By the end of this day cycle, the process will be complete. It would have been sooner, but your stunt with the Captain set you back a bit." She moves down to my chest, her marvelous fingers probing my skin and muscles.

Several of the tattoos on her hands, arms and throat are pulsing slowly. Comtats, that's what they're called. Command tattoos. *How did I know that? Wait. I remember. The 'lessons'. Man! The schools back home are in deep doodoo when this technology hits*!

The lesson memory dump kicks in and I 'remember' that every rank has a set of comtats that help them perform their jobs. They're like portable instruments and even weapons sometimes. You get more comtats as you learn your 'rate', which is your job in the Navy. You also enhance your comtats as you progress up the command structure. I can see intricate tattoo lines covering much of Nanel's shapely body, but only some of them are pulsing. *I wonder how much of her body has those almost invisible lines. Focus, Jake, focus.*

Wow. Wait, did she say age 25? I raise my hand slowly and look at it. The wrinkles are gone. The little shake is gone. I slowly look down my arms to my chest. The hairs on my arms and chest-- they're black. Not grey or white but glossy black. My gaze travels further south and... *Oh my God, where's my beer gut?*

Nanel has moved down to the private's privates just as I notice I have privates again. It's been a while since I could see over my beer belly. Her very thorough exam is bringing my usually silent partner to full attention for the first time in quite a while. I groan out loud before I realize it, "Damn, that feels good." I can feel my face turn into a tomato as I glance up at Nanel. Her smile is delicious. She moves on to exam my thighs and legs.

"Relax, recruit. This is common among your species. You'll find that as your body heals and finishes the rejuv process, you'll regain your physical and mental abilities. Your arousal is a good sign." She glances down and back up. "Consider this when you make your decision to stay or not," she says with a soft chuckle.

My species? "Um, ma'am. You said 'my species'. Aren't you human?" She looks incredibly human to me.

Nanel halts her probing, looks up at me and smiles. Then she looks back down and continues her methodical exam, working down each leg as she speaks. "No, Mr. Jasper, I'm not human. My species would best be described as bioandroid though that's not entirely correct. We are not manufactured like a true android. My species can self procreate and we biologically mature in stages from child to adult much like the human species. The act of mating is very similar to your human intercourse. If you are interested we can discuss this another time."

Uh, bio-android? Not human? Oh, I'm definitely going to discuss this with you later.

Something else hits me. *Nah, couldn't be.* "Excuse me if this is out of line, ma'am, but you bear a striking resemblance to one of the models in a calendar for…"

Nanel stops her probing and puts her hands on my knees, bending slightly. "Ridgid Tools, Mr. Jasper? March of 1967, I believe."

"Uh. Yes, ma'am. But…"

She stands and places her hands on her hips. "The crew is allowed R&R periodically, Mr. Jasper. How we choose to spend it is our business. I rather liked the photo, didn't you?" Those sparkling eyes are twinkling with amusement. "That is one of my fondest memories of Earth, Jake. It was a period when your culture was finally maturing a bit."

She taps my knee and turns to the console. "Stand please." Her fingers fly over the console, and the bed starts to move into the floor as I rise up. "Ship, I believe Mr. Jasper is sufficiently healed to finish the interface tests and tour the ship. If you concur, please use the implant interface."

Ship's voice sounds in my head again. "Testing is now complete, Surgeon. His interface is functioning normally."

Nanel turns to me and says, "Did you hear Ship internally or externally Mr. Jasper?"

"Most definitely in my head, ma'am. Loud and clear."

"Excellent," she says as she presses a comtat on her wrist. It glows green for a moment. "Bridge, Nanel. Status please."

"The Battle Squadron will be reformed within the hour, sir. All vessels repaired sufficiently to transit." The voice sounds not in my head but over the ship intercom again.

"Very well. Make preparations to transit as soon as possible. Contact me the moment we're ready. Inform the Captain of these orders. Nanel out."

"Well Recruit, we have less than an hour to convince you to serve and defend. Let's get started." To Arlo she says, "I'd like you to accompany Mr. Jasper. It's customary in cases where the recruit already has a partner." Arlo's little head tilts to one side, and I hear his voice, "Sure. It beats sitting around here twiddling my toes. Should Jake cover his new hairy hide, or is it normal here to walk around in your birthday suit?"

Her laugh is low and sweet. She points to a small alcove in the far wall. "Quite right, Arlo. Mr. Jasper, you'll find a uniform in the exam nook. Please dress quickly. Your tour starts now." She turns and walks through an opening that appears in the wall. This time it stays open.

Chapter Six

The uniform fits perfectly. It's a simple green, short sleeved tunic and matching pants. The pair of soft soled shoes reminds me of my deck shoes on the subs. The outfit reminds me of those hospital scrubs I see nurses wearing on the TV medical dramas, except these have military creases and seem to be starched, though they feel soft. I walk through the opening to join Nanel; Arlo is perched on my right shoulder. "Nice pajamas, Recruit," pipes Arlo as his eye does a couple of rolls.

We don't stop as Nanel looks up from one of her comtats, "You're on ship time now, Recruit, sloth is not allowed. Step onto my transport, please. I've enabled the handles."

This tile is much bigger than the last one and has something like a bicycle handlebar sticking up from the base. I grab the handle and immediately feel the pull of the field around my lower body. The tile rises, and we pick up speed quickly. We spin around the corridor just slowly enough for me to get a feel for the general layout of the ship as Nanel narrates.

"We're leaving the medical area, which is approximately amidships and surrounded by the weapons area. The ship is basically a series of layered torus shapes with a central transit shaft connecting them." We enter the huge central shaft I'd flown through before on the way to the bridge, and the tile slopes 'down'. It feels down anyway. I look behind me, and sure enough, I can see the bridge layer receding. *OK, it's a big stack of metal doughnuts. Not as sexy as a star destroyer, but they must have their reasons. I guess.*

"It's a simple and effective configuration meant for quick access to any section and to maximize our response to damage control. At least that is the designer's theory. Engineers are a strange lot. Don't you agree?" I swear she's smirking at me.

"Uh. I suppose so, ma'am. I was a software grunt for forty years, and I'd say 'interesting' fits better than 'strange'." It's a reflex reaction to the implied insult. At least I think it's a slam, I'm not sure.

"No, Mr. Jasper, it is not a 'slam'. Quite the opposite, I find the engineering intellect fascinating."

"Wait a minute; I didn't say that out loud." A chill runs down my spine as we whiz past the huge doughnut sections of the ship. "Are you telepathic like Arlo? I'm going to be in deep doodoo if everyone around here can read my thoughts."

"No, Mr. Jasper, not all the crew is telepathic, though some species are. That ability is generally only between a crewman and his partner. I hear your thoughts because you have not learned to toggle your implant. Ship is controlling your output so that only I can hear you through it until you gain control. Control of your implant will be part of your training."

She glances at me and gives me a smile that could melt an iron beam at 20 paces. "And thank you, Recruit. I work very hard to keep my body in shape." She turns forward again, her face alive with amusement. "Until you gain control, Ship will attempt to filter your thoughts through the implant, so you needn't be concerned with what I will hear."

Oh crap. Wait, can I say that now? Will she hear it? Crap, did she hear 'crap'. Arrggghh.

"At ease, Mr. Jasper," I recognize PIP's voice in my head. "As the Surgeon said, I am filtering your implant. You are not sending or receiving the normal communications with the rest of the crew. As of now, you can assume your thoughts are private unless you address me first, and direct me to allow you to speak through your implant to someone. Please try this now."

Ok. PIP, please uh, open a channel to, uh. How do I address her PIP? Is it Lieutenant Commander Nanel? Sir? Ma'am? What's the correct address?

"Sir or ma'am is usually the most direct and correct, Mr. Jasper. And you can say 'Contact Nanel' as a short phrasing. You will hear a tone when the connection is made and open."

Ok. PIP please contact Nanel. I heard a soft bell note. *Sir, testing, testing. ZZ Top rules!*

Nanel tilts her head in my direction, her smile broadens a bit. *Yes, Recruit, and I must say you are a 'sharp dressed man'. Now we* need to toggle your implant. I need to talk openly with you, and we don't have much time. Ship, toggle Mr. Jasper's implant for now.*

I hear another tone, and I can somehow tell that the connection with Nanel has been broken. *Good, it's very hard to concentrate on not concentrating on the beautiful woman, bio-android or not, riding next to me.* Her uniform is clinging in all the right places.

I can feel the tile slowing, and Nanel says, "I'm afraid a complete tour will have to wait, Recruit, I've just been called to the bridge. I will take you to the nearest crews' lounge and there we must determine your fate. I've contacted Chief Engineer Stokes to continue the interview."

The tile continues to slow as it zips into a side corridor from the main shaft. We flow past hundreds of crewmen; most look human but several are, I don't know, different. I can't really examine them at this speed. We turn into another corridor and move toward the 'outside' of the donut towards another set of screens.

The tile stops and the handle bars retract into the base. Nanel steps off the tile and starts towards what has to be the outer most surface of the ship on this level, passing by dozens of tables and chairs. I hustle to keep up, Arlo digging in to stay perched.

We stop a few feet in front of a screen. I look left and right. In fact, we're standing two feet from what looks like the edge of a cliff curving behind us, the dark void of space inches from my face. I cautiously put my hand out to touch the screen. It isn't a screen; it's some kind of invisible field. Where I touch it little swirls of color radiate out. I can't push through it but it feels like some kind of thick, pliable, clear plastic.

"It's a containment field, Recruit. You'll learn about the technology if you stay with us." She brings a hand close to her mouth and touches one of her comtats. "Mr. Stokes, I have Mr. Jasper in crew's lounge 22. Will you be joining us this year?" Her voice is stern, but I can tell the reprimand is light.

"I'm 30 seconds away Nanel. There is a ship to run, you know." The voice sounds as though it is right next to us. A male voice! *So this isn't a ship of Amazons after all. I'm not sure if that's good or bad.*

"Chief Engineer Stokes will be able to answer your immediate question, I believe. Do you have any questions for me before he arrives?" Her pose is relaxed, but I can tell she is thinking about other things.

I look at this amazing woman standing next to me and have a sudden epiphany. "Where were you recruited from, sir?"

She turns to me with a sad smile. "Ah. You have empathy as well as intelligence. I like that in a crewman." She turns to look back out into the void. "I like it in a man, as well, Mr. Jasper." The hint is obvious, so my next question is obvious as well.

"Since you're diverting my question, I'll assume it's none of my business for now. Your last comment confuses me though. Can I take a leap of faith and assume there is no law against crewmen being, ah, in relationships? In my Navy, that is strictly a no-no. Bad for crew morale and all that baloney." The sad look is slowly replaced with a nice, girl next door smile and a tilt of her head.

"There is no regulation against relationships here, Mr. Jasper. Our moral standards are quite high though. We do not tolerate violence or abuse, in any form, against other crewmen. The penalties are quite severe. But we understand and encourage interactions that make life worth living."

She adds, "You will find most species in the FTG are socially mature, Jake. It comes mostly from realizing that every life is unique and precious to us all. We don't have the time or energy to spare on petty differences and false pretenses."

Nanel glances behind me. "Ah, I see Mr. Stokes has finally graced us with an appearance." A tall man in a crisp green uniform steps off a tile before it even stops.

Turning back to me, Nanel offers, "If you decide to enlist, Jake, I hope we'll be able to be friends as well as shipmates. For now, it's time for my watch to begin." She gives Arlo's little head a stroke and then reaches out her hand for me to shake.

I take her cool, smooth hand in mine. Her grip is firm but feminine. Her smile melts my kneecaps. Turning to the other man in the room, her voice becomes crisp and formal again. "Mr. Stokes this is Recruit Jasper. He is from Earth and has very little time to make his enlistment decision. I'll leave him in your care to finish the interview." Stokes nods and steps to the side to let her walk by. It takes all my will not to linger on her swaying derriere. I look up at the smiling face of Mr. Stokes, who has his hand extended for me to shake. *Oops.*

"Relax, Mr. Jasper. I know how difficult it is to turn off the hormones with creatures like her around. But we have only a few minutes before you have to make a very difficult and potentially life-changing decision." He motions to one of the tables closest to the screen. "Let's sit and have something to drink. I believe humans drink coffee as a stimulant, is that correct?" We sit in the small, comfortable chairs, facing out into the dark void.

The surface of the table glows under his hand as he taps a symbol. "One coffee and one stiox, please." He must have noticed me staring out at space just beyond the screen. "It's a little overwhelming at first, I know." I turn back to face him. "We grabbed you from your normal life on Earth and thrust you directly into a pitched battle in deep space. That's got to shake up anyone's day." His smile is genuine and understanding.

He turns to the creature bringing our drinks. At first she looks human, but the short light brown fur is a definite give away. "Gentlemen. Enjoy." She sits the drinks on the table, and I see that her hands are very delicate and very lethal. Her nails are more like thin knives, at least four inches long. Her eyes have a cat like quality and are a brilliant green with flecks of yellow. Her grey uniform is more like an apron, barely covering her slim figure. She flashes me a quick smile, providing a clear view of her pointed white teeth and bright pink tongue. *My first alien, and I meet a she-cat.* Arlo slinks around my neck to the far shoulder. *Easy, buddy, she only looks like a cat.*

"Easy for you to say, you don't look like a snack to her."

I turn back to Stokes and take up my mug of steaming coffee. I take a sip. It's delicious! It reminds me of how coffee tasted the first time I had it, rich, creamy and thick. I raise my eyebrows, "Is it my imagination, or does this taste extraordinarily good?"

Stokes laughs, "No, Mr. Jasper, it's because of your recent rejuv. The short story is that rejuv will keep your body at your prime life-age, which includes nerve sensitivity among other things. You will need to rejuv at intervals and, of course, if you are injured. While you enjoy your drink let me give you the enlistment speech. No questions until I'm done. Is that agreed?" He sits back in his chair with his arms folded, waiting for my response.

"Yes sir."

He relaxes and sits forward. "Excellent. Here we go. It's short and sweet Mr. Jasper. You've been recruited to replace a crewman recently killed in battle." He coughs into his hand, trying to hide his emotions. "Mr. Griff was one of my best analysts, and an excellent engineer. He was also a close friend of mine and will be sorely missed." I can see he's trying hard not to think about this lost crewman.

"You are one of a select few humans we have been following that meet our recruitment standards. You're single, widowed I believe. I'm sorry for your loss. You have no immediate attachments to your world, other than three grown daughters, whom you rarely see. Your experience in your planet's Navy and your software skills in civilian life are ideal for the position. Your software research and patent for interfacing with artificial intelligences makes you a prime candidate."

Stokes takes a sip of his drink and continues, "An analysis of your DNA shows you have a strong constitution, a robust immune system and, most importantly, you will respond well to the rejuv process." He takes another sip and leans back, looking at me intensely. "The Executive Officer and her team had screened your aptitude results months ago as part of our 'Ready Recruit' program. You scored quite well in all aspects except one." He peers down into his drink for a moment and then back up to me. "You have a somewhat, shall we say 'odd' attitude towards authority." He leans forward to ask me, "Can you tell me why you went to a Captain's Mast hearing on your first submarine deployment?"

Damn, how do they know about that? It was supposed to be stricken from my records! But thinking back on that scene makes me smile. I know exactly what he's talking about. It was Chief Buttface's rant outside the Maneuvering Room. It was my first watch after qualifying onboard the Bluefish, and the Auxiliary Chief decided he would come back to the Engineering spaces and puff up his ego on the new guy: me. "Yes, sir, it's one of my fondest memories in fact. I was standing my first fully qualified watch in engineering when Chief Butt... I mean Bufaccia, the forward Auxiliary Chief Petty Officer, decided to take out his frustrations on me. It seems one of the aft engineering officers had found an auxiliary petty officer asleep on watch and chewed him out. Chief Buffacia came aft and told me he was going to perform a spot inspection of the engineering spaces since the officer had harassed one of his men." I sit up a little in my chair. It still riles me after 40 years. "I was standing outside Maneuvering, talking to the RO, the Reactor Operator."

Stokes smiles and says, "And was your response respectful and in line with military protocol, Mr. Jasper?"

I cough a little and decide it's better to just be me than pretending to be someone I'm not. "I told Chief Buttface that of course he could inspect my spaces, but, as he was not qualified on any of the equipment, he was not to turn any valves or flip any switches." *Well that's it then, he'll be walking me out the recruitment backdoor now.* I wait for the swift reprimand and dismissal I'm sure is coming. In my experience, an officer is an officer no matter which Navy it is, and the good ones are much too rare.

Chief Stokes sits back heavily in his chair with a stunned look. I'm waiting for him to call the MPs or the red-suited Marine dudes. Then his face contorts into a wide smile. He barks out a loud laugh, slapping a hand on his thigh. He quickly composes himself and looks around. "That seems more than a bit disrespectful and presumptuous of you, Mr. Jasper. Perhaps you deserved your mast after all." I can tell he's waiting for me to defend myself.

Fine. In for a penny and all that crap. "Perhaps I did, sir. But I believe that respect is earned not given or bought. Chief Butt... I mean Chief Bufaccia did not deserve my respect The uniform he wore did. The chief was an arrogant asshole, abusing his rank because one of his men was derelict in his duties, and the chief was embarrassed. I tried to earn respect everyday in everything I did, and I expected everyone else onboard to do the same."

Chief Stokes is silent for a moment and then stands and motions for me to follow him. "I'll want to hear more of your time on station, Mr. Jasper. For now let's get to Engineering for a quick tour." *OK. Is the exit door in Engineering?*

Three short, loud, irritating buzzes blare in the lounge intercom, and then we hear, "Chief Stokes. Report to Core Control immediately." At the same time, I see the chief reach for his comtat.

"What's the problem, Core?" He is already heading for his tile.

"We're having trouble stabilizing the containment fields, Chief. I need help keeping this jury rig from flying apart."

The Chief looks at me and then points to a table in the far corner. It's occupied with another cat girl intent on some kind of screen on her table. "Lieutenant Tisp." Cat Girl turns to the chief and nods.

"Yes, Chief?"

"I need you to babysit this recruit until I return. Don't damage him, he hasn't enlisted yet." He turns, mounts the tile and disappears through the wall in the blink of an alien's bug-eye.

Cat Girl adjusts her seat towards me, crosses an incredibly shapely set of legs and raises a decidedly feline eyebrow. "Well, Recruit? Don't be shy. I will bite but not until you enlist. Come sit, and we'll discuss philosophy or whatever else pops up." Her smile is inviting, and more than a little predatory.

Chapter Seven

Uh. Damage? Hey, Arlo, you see a way out of this? I'm getting some bad vibes about Cat Woman over there.

I notice that this time Arlo hasn't shied away from the cat lady. "No way, Jake. Take a gander at her partner on the table. That's Leeta. We've been snoogling while you made with the blah, blah, blah crap. Get your sorry ass over there and make nice with Tisp." Arlo's tail smacks the back of my neck and he's almost bouncing up and down. "Giddy up, cowboy, I want to get up close and personal with Leeta."

Fine. It's time to get more perspective on our situation anyway. I saunter over to the table. By saunter I mean I try to act casual and cool. It probably looks more like a bad moon walk in reverse.

Tisp motions to the seat across the table, and I sit my silly ass down with as much machismo as I can muster. "Excuse me, ma'am. Sorry you have to babysit Arlo and me. I'm sure you have better things to do." At this point, Arlo smacks my head again. "Oh. Sorry. This is Arlo, my partner."

Tisp smiles again, seeming to enjoy my discomfort. She strokes the tail of the striking orange chameleon sitting on the table. "Relax, Recruit, I was only kidding about the biting remark. This is Leeta, my partner. I believe she and Arlo have been getting to know each other while you were talking to Chief Stokes."

"Yes, we surely were, Mr. Jasper." I hear Leeta's sweet southern drawl echo in my head. "Would you two mind if Arlo and I moseyed over there and had our own little tete-a-tete?" And without waiting for Tisp or me to respond, Leeta and Arlo head for the far side of the table. I figure they'll get there sometime in August.

"Um. Seems like we're on our own, Recruit," purrs Tisp as she turns her legs back under the table. She leans forward, setting an elbow on the table and resting her gorgeous face in her hand. She runs her deep pink, pointed tongue around her lips. Her other hand starts a slow tap of her four inch nails. "What shall we talk about?"

An awkward moment passes. Suddenly she sits back and lets out a thoroughly delightful, full bodied laugh. "Please forgive me, Mr.

Jasper. It was too good of an opportunity to pass up. I'm neither predatory nor hungry." She looks me up and down slowly and adds, "Though I'll admit, I'm withholding judgment for a later date. Come on, Mr. Jasper, you have my undivided attention. What would you like to know?"

I let out a sigh of relief. "Whew. For a moment there I thought I might not make it to my interview in one piece!"

"I'll warn you that if you make any 'cat' jokes at this stage, you may not, Recruit. I'm aware of the resemblance of my species to your domesticated felines."

"Yes, ma'am, I'll do my best. May I ask what species you are?"

"We're called Talusha, my home planet is Taluss. Leeta and I have been partners for quite some time. Leeta is a panther chameleon from your planet, Earth."

That takes me aback. "So obviously you've been to Earth before. How long ago was that?"

"Over two hundred years ago, Jake."

My surprise must show on my face, or the fact that my jaw is bouncing off the deck. Tisp purrs again and says, "Don't spoil it for Arlo. Let him find out on his own. Leeta will enjoy his reaction as much as I'm enjoying yours."

"Oh, I wouldn't spoil that surprise for all the tea in China."

I look over at Arlo. He's just kind of slowly bouncing up and down in time with Leeta. I wonder what they're talking about. Does he know his lizard lady is really a cougar?

Tisp continues, "So. Let's put that aside, shall we? You'll learn all about the rejuv process if you sign up. So what else can I tell you?"

I look back at the silky-faced officer across the table. *OK. Here we go.* "How long has this war been going on, Tisp? And how did it start? And why doesn't Earth know about it?" I stop and smile, realizing I'm firing question after question. "Sorry, ma'am, there is just so much I want to know."

"I understand Mr. Jasper, and I'll answer what I can. But for some of your questions you'll need to visit the librarian, it's just too much information for you to process verbally."

That catches me off guard. "Librarian? I thought the ship's AI controlled the vessel."

"Ah. That's a common recruit mistake, Mr. Jasper." She purrs softly. Yes purrs. I'm not making this stuff up. "Since we're both off-duty and in a casual environment, let's drop the formalities, shall we? My name is Meesha." She extends her hand, and the nails retract back to only one inch long.

Her hand is firm and very soft; the fur is incredibly fine. "I'm Jake, Meesha. Jake Jasper. Thank you. It's very kind of you to try and put me at ease." I gaze around at the tables and back to this incredible being. "I'm sure this is not what you were planning to do with your time in the lounge today."

She drops her hand back to one knee. "No, it's not. I was studying the latest Intel on GHA activities in this quadrant." She motions to the tablet. It looks like a clear sheet of thick glass with diagrams, text and images scrolling around. Even from my angle, I can see that the images extend out several inches in front of the surface, giving them a three dimensional effect.

"To answer one of your questions at least, I'm communicating with the Librarian using this interface pad. Normally we use a holo room dedicated to library interactions, but I don't need full immersion for this work."

"So the Library is controlled by a different AI from the ship AI?"

"Yes. The Ship AI must be dedicated to monitoring and controlling all aspects of Triumphs' thousands of functioning systems. To distract it from those activities with library functions is inefficient. Especially considering the depth of abilities the Library is capable of. You will understand better when you're allowed full access to your Librarian. For now consider what it takes to contain, search and provide access to the combined data of thousands of species."

Of course! Thinking back on my last AI project, I'm beginning to understand the reasoning of separating the AIs. "I get it, Tisp. I can't wait to see what kind of user interface your library AI provides. That was one of my areas of research before they pulled the plug."

"Pulled the plug?" She looks at me quizzically, and then taps on the pad in front of her for a few seconds. "Ah. You lost your financial backing for a project. Is that correct?"

"Wow. That was fast. Is manual natural language interfacing the only way to access the Library?" I could see a keypad display at the bottom of the pad screen but its symbols looked like a cross between Arabic, Chinese and hen scratching.

"Of course not. But sometimes working this way helps me focus my thoughts and is faster than the full immersion interface."

This is too tempting to let pass. "Is there any reason I can't use the Library now? I have to wait for Chief Stokes to get back before I can continue my interview and you're busy with your own work."

Tisp looks to her left at a small alcove next to the 'bar' and back to me. "There's a Library Nook right there. The ship has thousands of them, placed wherever a crewman might need immersive information or recreation."

Uh, recreation? Hmm, I'll save that question for later. "Why not let me visit the Library for a few minutes? It might help me make up my mind about enlisting." OK, that was stretching a little, but I'm getting excited about seeing what they have for a holodeck interface.

Tisp licks her tiny, pink tongue over her upper lip, smiling. "You're very convincing, Recruit. Actually, a visit to the Library would be a much faster way to get a lot of your questions answered." She raises a finger to hold off any more questions. "Ship, I'd like to introduce Recruit Jasper to his Librarian. Is that within his current enlistment parameters?"

"Yes, Lieutenant Tisp. Chief Stokes would have given Mr. Jasper a tour of a Library Alcove at some point. Shall I make the lounge alcove available?" A small blue light above the alcove in the corner starts blinking softly.

"Yes. I'll accompany Mr. Jasper and acquaint him with standard protocol. Please limit his access to 10 minutes." She rises gracefully from the chair. "Please follow me, Mr. Jasper. You can bring Arlo if he wants. He can experience the interface through your link." She turns and slinks towards the wall alcove.

"You want in on this, Arlo?" I say looking at the other table. Arlo and Leeta are still doing the slow mambo.

"Not a chance, Jake. Leeta and I are still getting to know each other. You go have fun in your stuffy old library; I'll be here when you get back." Dang, he didn't even pivot a beady eye at me. That little lizard is smitten!

"Fine. Don't miss me too much." Sheesh.

Meesha is waiting beside the tiny entrance. Inside I can see a comfy-looking chair with a silver halo thingy above the head. "Have a seat Mr. Jasper. I'll get back to my intel while you're getting familiar with the Library. Just say 'enter library' to start the interface. A privacy screen will cloak you once you engage. You can disengage at any point just by saying 'leave library'."

I settle into the chair and get my first shock as it seems to be alive, moving and forming around my body. It's like having tiny fingers gently massage you all over. Very nice.

"You'll have ten minutes, use your time wisely, Recruit." Tisp turns and walks back towards her table. *That is one fine feline derriere. Damn, how does any male on this ship get any work done? Maybe I'll ask the Librarian.*

"Enter library." A hazy film hides my view of Meesha's talents and then the second shock; the face of an elderly woman with silver hair and thick black glasses forms about eye level where the opening was. The voice comes through my implant, and damn if doesn't sound like it's already caught me talking too loud.

"Yes, Recruit? How can I help you?"

Now what do I do? "Huh, what do I call you? 'Librarian' seems a little formal."

I think she actually sniffs before answering. "Well. You could create a moniker for library access just as you did 'PIP' for the Ship. What moniker would you like? Analyzing your conversations since you boarded, I can recommend several avatars such as this one." Shock three is seeing last month's Playmate standing in front of me with her silk blouse unbuttoned down to the navel, a black pleated mini-shirt and five inch red heels. Her bleach blonde hair is loosely tied up in a bun on her head. *Oh my God, am I that transparent?*

"Is this acceptable or do you have another image in mind?" The avatar's lips move with the Librarian's voice. It's slowly shifting from foot to foot, the blouse threatening to burst from the pressure.

"No. No. As much as I enjoy this uh, avatar, I don't think I'd be able to concentrate on anything if I tried to talk to it." OK, I don't want to talk to the wicked witch of the west either so what's a good librarian 'avatar'? Got it! "Let's try Einstein, Library."

The bodacious blonde is replaced by a frumpy little man with shocks of white hair, and a pipe. "I assume you are referring to Albert Einstein, born March 14th, 1879 in Wurttemberg, Germany, Earth. Famous theoretical physicist. Winner of the 1921 Nobel Peace Prize of Physics, creator of the formula…"

"Yes. Yes. Perfect." *I should have no distraction issues with this avatar.* "So, Einstein, can I access you just like I do PIP, just think your name?"

The shaggy head nods as it removes the smoking pipe. "Exactly, Mr. Jasper. As a crewman, you'll have audio access at any time. I can also provide low resolution three dimensional imagery if you access through a tablet or if you are near an instrument console. I can provide you with limited enhanced mental lessons as you've already experienced."

"Tisp mentioned a 'full immersion' interface. What is that, and how do I access it?"

Einstein points the pipe in my direction as he says, "Ah, now that is the best possible way to comprehend some information, especially complex data and concepts. What you are experiencing now is only part of my capabilities." He tilts his head and continues, "I've just verified with Ship that you are cleared to create your personal library for this session."

"I don't understand. Isn't this my personal library?"

"No, Mr. Jasper, this is just the standard library alcove session. We've found that presenting the crewman with a familiar environment for study greatly enhances the immersion experience. I have an Earth environment in data storage if you would like to try it. We've already consumed two of your ten minute allotment."

Crap, I forgot about Meesha's warning. "Yes. Let's go with that one. Can I change it later?"

"If you enlist, Mr. Jasper, you may experiment with the immersion experience as you see fit. I'm engaging the standard Earth library environment now."

The alcove morphs into a rich, dark paneled, English mansion study. My chair is now a deep, ox-blood red leather cloud. I can smell the musky tanned hide scent of quality leather and something else; something sharp, woody and alcoholic. Scotch! In my right hand is a clinking glass of rich golden liquid! In my left hand is a warm Meerschaum pipe with fragrant smoke curling up. I'm wearing a red smoking jacket, black slacks and a comfortable pair of fuzzy bunny slippers.

A slow glance around the dark teak wood room confirms my suspicions. Between the floor to ceiling shelves of rich bound books are magnificent paintings of early Playmates. I knew this library looked familiar.

"We are just under three minutes into your session, Mr. Jasper. Perhaps you should concentrate on your questions." Einstein appears in a chair across from me. *This is going to take some getting used to, but damn it's cool!*

"Right. OK." I'm trying to phrase the best questions. *Crap, I'm going to waste more time doing that. Forget it! Just go for the high level stuff!* "Fine. How and when did this war start?"

The room twists and morphs, and suddenly I'm whizzing through space, passing whirling galaxies, nebulas and other astronomical thingies I can't remember from school. "We're traveling to the first border dispute recorded, Mr. Jasper. Its location is classified above your pay grade for now. This is a reenactment of an event that occurred roughly 1,200 of your solar years ago."

The whizzing stops and I'm standing inside the control room of some kind of huge orbital construction platform, looking out into space. I'm surrounded by a nightmarish collection of interconnected struts, beams and weird globes of some blue-gray metal. Below the platform horizon I can see a beautiful reddish brown planet dotted with what must be huge lakes, and interconnecting rivers.

Einstein says, "This is the planet P'ashna Zoep, where the war began. There were about 5,000 planets already in the fledgling 'Galactic Alliance' The Alliance included peaceful species of all type, including aquatic. Representatives of the GHA had made initial contact, and asked for a treaty meeting in Alliance space."

The enormous red and green lumpy 'rocks' are approaching the platform. There must be hundreds of them, all different shapes and sizes. The screen in front of us flips from the scene in space to the image of a hideous octopus-looking creature, like a splotchy bloated red bag floating in some kind of bubbling gel.

"The GHA envoy proposed sending 5 'peace' ships to the meeting, so the Alliance had deployed 5 research ships and the Admiral's flag ship, 'H'Not', around the platform in a show of respect for the treaty."

"Uh, Einstein, I'd say there are at least two hundred of those overgrown barnacles. And I'd say they are arranged in a classic battle grouping. I'm getting a feeling that this will not end up well for the fledging whatever."

"Your instincts are correct, Mr. Jasper. The conversation was recorded for posterity but this scene is reconstructed from what little remained of the ship recorders, and what we knew of the GHA at the time."

The monstrous image raises a tentacle, and brings it down in a slicing motion. "R'tic!" The garbled screech booms in the platform's intercom. Instantly all the grotesque rocks around the platform erupt with bright streaks of red and white beams, targeting the Galactic Alliance research ships and the platform. It's over in seconds. The H'Not was unable to return fire before it was vaporized.

The scene dissolves, and I'm back in my comfy chair, breathing heavily. Einstein is puffing on his pipe with his hands in his lap. "There were no survivors. The planet was aquaformed immediately after the ambush. And, unfortunately for the Galactic Alliance, this scenario was repeated three more times before the Alliance Council stopped seeking peace and declared war."

I stopped to take this in. *Gigantic Octo-Baddies; 1,200 years; ambushing peace envoys. Got it.* "How many planets have been lost to the GHA squids since the war began?"

Einstein stands and waves his hand. The room morphs back into the alcove. The avatar is standing in front of me now. "I'm sorry Mr. Jasper but your time has expired. Lieutenant Tisp is waiting for you. Please disengage the library now." And poof, he's gone.

"Leave library," I say. The chair tilts up and releases me, its surface smooth again. The haze by the entrance vanishes, and there stands Meesha, one arm on the alcove and the other propped on a shapely hip. She's tapping a long fingernail against the edge of the alcove, smiling that 'cat got your tongue' smile. No, really, I swear. She's sliding her tongue across her top lip, what else am I supposed to think?

"Well, I hope you used your time wisely, Recruit. Chief Stokes will be here in five." We start back toward our table; my head is spinning with more questions than answers. *It's time to find out more about this stunning cat woman.*

"Meesha, I'd like to ask about your home planet…"

Three loud, sharp blasts of an alarm sound over the intercom. "All hands. All hands. Report to transit stations. Report to transit stations. This is not a drill. Report to transit stations. Transit in 20 seconds."

The alarm repeats, and Tisp is off like a shot. She grabs Leeta off the table then hurries towards a tile. "Sorry, Jake. Talk's over for now. Stay here. Someone will be back for you as soon as possible." She taps a comtat and says, "Ship. Quarantine Mr. Jasper and his partner to this compartment, and monitor him." Without looking back she speeds through the opening, her tile diving down the shaft. The door disappears but the alarm continues. I turn to the outer screens wondering what the hell is happening.

"Hey Arlo. Buddy. You still hear me?" Arlo has walked back across the table to sit on the top of a chair. He turns his little head, and focuses the nearest eye on me.

"Yes, 'Partner'. I grokked all of it. We're screwed, blued and tattooed if you ask me."

"Transit in 5 seconds. Prepare to fold." The alarm shifts to a soft, slow 'boop, boop, boop', and time seems to slow to a crawl. I can feel something in my gut start to twist. *Oh my God.* Arlo is vibrating from his nose to the tip of his tail. Both his eyes are fixed forward, looking out at space.

"Uh, have you noticed that the stars are gone, Jake?" His voice is slowing down with each boop, booop, boooop.

It feels like hours for me to spin around, and to look out the screen. No stars; no light of any kind. Not even a faint haze of distant galaxies. *Crap. I wonder what 'fold' means?*

Chapter Eight

The soft booping sound speeds back up and then stops. I feel like my insides are going to become my outsides. The intercom sounds again, "Transit complete." Instantly, my gut snaps back in place like a greasy rubber band. Arlo has stopped vibrating but he's crouched low on the chair gripping it for dear life with his funky little feet.

"Are you ok, Arlo? Talk to me, buddy." I reach down to check on my cold blooded partner. He snaps his left eye towards me, and back to the screen.

"Jake, check it out! The stars are back!" Arlo is sort of jerking up and down a little on his tiny little legs. His tongue is flicking in and out excitedly. And considering how Arlo uses that sticky lasso it's pretty weird looking.

Walking closer to the view screen, it's easy to see there are stars alright. And lots of other bright objects, including some that are exploding under the onslaught of colored energy beams and missiles everywhere. *I've seen this movie before. Damn!*

"Arlo, we're going into battle again. Jeez, don't these people ever take a break?" I look around at the lounge. Other than the smooth walls and tables it's empty. *Great, not even the cat girl waitress to talk to.*

"Arlo, can you hear anything from the ship or any other partners talking?"

"Nada, Jake, just your slightly hysterical voice in my head. Leeta said she'd meet me later if there was a later. Then my head was empty again. Damn, please let there be a later, Jake, Leeta's a hottie."

"I've got my fingers crossed for us, Arlo, trust me."

Arlo snaps his eye to the screen and back to me. "I think we're on our own for now. Any idea where the bathroom is, I need to go." He's looking around the lounge, his eyes rotating in truly weird directions.

"Uh, no. I'd say any old corner would do in an emergency, buddy."

Arlo bounces down the chair and saunters off. Arlo doesn't 'run' anywhere. A saunter is his top speed, so I know he's desperate. I know how he feels, I'm lucky I don't need a uniform change myself.

The scene outside is shifting, ships dancing about to some unheard fiddler. The Triumph seems to be moving into position with some other huge ships but it's really hard to tell without a frame of reference. And of course there's no sound, just brilliant explosions. It's impossible to tell which ka-booms are ours and which are theirs. The beams of colored mist and lights are everywhere.

I need to do something. I can't just sit here waiting for the next ka-boom to be us. How can I get the Ship to talk to me? *Crap, what did I call the ship's AI? Oh, right.*

"PIP. Can you read me, Ship? I want to connect or link or whatever the friggin right term is. I wanna talk to you, damn it!"

I hear the soft tone in my head. "How may I help you, Mr. Jasper? We are a bit busy at the moment, as I'm sure you can see."

"That's just it, PIP. I can't sit here and just watch. I want to help. What can I do to help?" I know it sounds ludicrous, but I can't help myself. I've never worked well with the 'stay here and wait for orders' kind of environment. Go figure.

"You haven't even been through basic training, Mr. Jasper. I doubt you can be of any help at this point. Please remain calm. I can shield the viewport if the sight of the battle is disturbing you." The view screen begins to turn white, blocking out the scene outside.

"No. Please don't block the view. I'm not afraid of the battle; I just need to do something. I can't just sit by like a lump on a log. Do you understand?"

The view returns. "I've restored the view, but you are not authorized to participate as a recruit, other than observe from the Battle Net."

"Wait, wait, PIP. Observe what; from where? What is the battle net?" I can feel my heart start to race.

"You could use the ship-wide Battle Network to observe the current battle from here. I would need your permission to link you to the training holosys. Since you've had no training in that link you might not be able to maintain the interface, and I cannot assist you further. Do you wish to attempt the link?"

My heart is pounding. I can see through the screen that we're getting closer to the action. I can almost make out the outlines of ships. I have to do something; I can't just wait for the Triumph, along with Arlo and me, to become space dust. "Yes, PIP. Link me into the net."

"Very well, Mr. Jasper. This may be a bit disorientating at first, please stand by."

King Kong slaps me upside the back of the head, and then shoves my face inside a video game machine, then wham, instant vertigo. Suddenly I'm outside the ship, looking down at Triumph from at least 100 feet above it; except I can't see my body. My girly scream echoes in my ears. "Ahhhh! What the frack! PIP, PIP, where am I?"

"You are linked to the Battle Net, Mr. Jasper. If you are experiencing extreme disorientation I can close the link."

"No. No. I can handle it. Just give me a minute.*" I am NOT going to blow this.* I focus on the ship. *It's ok; this is a simulation, man. It's not real. Or rather it is real but I'm not really outside. Ah crap, I have no idea what it is but I'm not going to bail.* "I'm good, PIP. I can handle this. What exactly am I seeing here?"

"My sensors and battle control are feeding you a simulation of our current situation report, our 'sitrep'. You are experiencing the battle as I see it. You have limited movement within the sim, since you are not yet qualified on this system."

My queasiness leaves me as I realize I can 'move' around. It's like I'm in my body, and there's a wacked out Virtual Reality helmet on my head. Turning to my left causes me to spin like a top around my position above the ship, the stars and ships whizzing by in a whir. I jerk my head back forward to stop my spin. *OK, got to be careful how fast I turn or lunch will be returning unannounced.*

The ship is definitely 'below' me, and I can't see through it to the other side of the ship. *Ok. Let's stretch our legs a little here.* I lean forward like I'm going to walk around the ship. The view instantly shifts, and I'm moving at Mach 20 around the ship.

"Whoa. Slow down, slow down, Jake, I'm going to lose my lunch here." It's Arlo's voice and he sounds pretty shaky.

"Hey, buddy. Are you seeing this, buddy? Is this a hoot or what?" I look around slowly but I can't see his scaly little face. "Where are you, buddy?"

"I'm outside the ship just like you, dumb shit, where do you think I am? You're the one who asked the Ship to link us up to this over grown Atari game. I got pulled along for the ride. Pay attention, Dude, you're about to face plant into that doohickey."

PIP's voice pipes in, "Your partner is linked in because of your telepathic link. You are doing quite well, Mr. Jasper."

"Thanks." I lean back to stop again at my 100 foot level, and now I can see the bridge below me. I lean slightly forward trying to move closer to the clear dome. *Yes!* I'm getting the hang of moving around slowly. I maneuver; ok I stumble, closer to the bridge deck. I can see the Captain standing next to her chair. Buzzing around her there are dozens of crewmen, all intent on the panels and screens surrounding the bridge.

"Can they see me, PIP?"

"Not by default, that would be too distracting. There are other observers on Battle Net, using this facility to monitor and assist in the battle."

The scene around us feels like it is expanding; the dots and flashes are getting larger and more frequent. There are groups of ships of all sizes performing a three dimensional, frenzied dance around us.

"PIP, it looks like we're getting closer to the action, but I can't tell which ships are the good guys." Instantly several of the ships in the distance are circled in bright red, the rest in blue.

"You will learn how to filter and process the Battle Net imaging during training, Mr. Jasper. I've enabled your view to show the GHA ships circled in red." Now the scene is making more sense. I see the groupings of ships, diving and maneuvering all around us. We're on the fringe of the battle, but I have a feeling that's about to change.

A thought occurs to me. "PIP, are you in communication with the AI's in our other ships?"

"Very perceptive, Mr. Jasper. Yes. The fleet AI's are in constant communication with each other. We assist in battle tactics and analysis. After your training, you'll be able to communicate with other ship AI's through me. You would be overwhelmed if we attempted that now."

I look into the bridge through the screens. The Captain is barking orders to the crew around her. Suddenly the bridge looks like someone stuck a stick down an ant hill.

Arlo pipes up, "Did you see the Captain just now, mate? I think the shit is about to hit the fan."

"Standby, Mr. Jasper," PIP warns. A moment later the AI says, "We've just been ordered to take a squadron and target an enemy position. For now you'll have to stay where you are while I assist."

Arlo's voice erupts into a Texas yell. "Yee haa, pard'. Hold onto to your saddle horn, it's time to ride!" *Great. Now I've got a crazed cowboy for a mental sidekick.*

Chapter Nine

There are more ships maneuvering to our sides and aft. At least I think it's aft. It feels aft. *Does my aft look too big in this hologram?*

"PIP, can I listen in on communications on the bridge, so I can tell what's happening? I feel like a deaf man at a Stones concert out here." I can sense that we're about to do something, I just can't tell what.

"I cannot interrupt the bridge at this time for such a request, Mr. Jasper."

I need to hear what is going on so I try again. "PIP. Chief Stokes was giving me a tour. Wouldn't I have been able to train on something like this as part of the tour?"

"Yes, that is consistent with our training program. Stand by. I will translate for you, Mr. Jasper."

"… as soon as the squadron has formed, Deck Officer. I want a Delta formation, Triumph at the point." I can see Captain Starla standing next to her chair, talking to another officer. "Transmit Admiral Izzac's orders and the coordinates for the target ship."

The Officer of the Deck replies, "All ships of the squadron have received and confirmed orders sir. We're waiting for the BlueSky and the Xsnix to maneuver into formation. Why this target, sir?"

"It's been tagged as a new ship type, an unknown. We're to change that classification, Deck. Now kick those ships into position, I want to move in 30 seconds."

"Aye, Captain. Attention Bluesky and Xsinix, attention. We are getting underway in 15 seconds, with or without you." The DO turns to left and commands, "Helm, make ready to take the squadron to target Alpha at full speed." Snapping to attention, she swivels to the Captain. "The board shows ready to maneuver, sir. All ships in formation."

"Very well, Deck Officer, best speed to target Alpha." She presses a comtat on the side of her neck. "Triumph squadron this is Triumph Prime. Prepare to engage target Alpha. This is an unknown enemy ship type. I want full spectrum, continuous scanning by all ships. Do not fire on Alpha unless fired upon. You may engage any other enemy ships that interfere. I want to know everything we can about this ship before we destroy it." Captain Starla glances around and then says, "Triumph engage."

Instantly I feel the ship swerve towards a distant speck. Looking around I can see a dozen other ships moving with us, in a kind of pyramid formation, with our ship at the apex. Arlo sounds off a wee bit too excitedly. "Tighten your cinches, cowboy, we're riding to glory! Yeeee Haaa!"

"It's not glory if your big bits end up as lots of little bits, bonehead! Keep quiet; I still don't have the hang of this damn simulator." When the Triumph veered off, I was caught off guard, and now I'm spinning off the side at 100 feet again. I concentrate on leaning back towards the bridge, and this time I get there within seconds. *Nice*.

"Well done, Recruit. You seem to have an aptitude for simulations." PIP's voice actually seems pleased. Just how sophisticated are these AIs? The talk from the bridge is a constant voice in my head, it takes all my concentration to watch the scene and understand what's going on.

"Yeah, all those years of playing of video games is paying off." I 'look' around and notice the squadron is still in that tight formation, and we're all accelerating. The simulation must be adding some tactile feedback, because I can 'feel' us swerve again, changing course.

Looking forward, I can see the red circled ships; some seem stationary, others dart around like angry bees. The ship directly in front of us is now the size of a pea, and growing fast. There are a dozen or so smaller dots in formation around it. "Is that our target, PIP?"

"Yes, Mr. Jakes. The enemy ship seems to have noticed our approach, it is changing course to intercept us." Even as PIP is talking I notice the red dots arcing around, coming towards us. From the target and the smaller dots around it I notice tiny flashes. *Uh oh*.

A strident voice from the bridge says, "Incoming missiles from target squadron! At least thirty missiles, locked on to our advance. All targeted on the Triumph."

"Steady as she goes, helm. Mr. Brocko, deploy defensive shields and countermeasures. Squadron offensive maneuver Zeta-Zeta-Two, repeat Zeta-Zeta-Two. All ships engage the target support ships; Triumph will engage the primary target. All Intel stations put sensors on maximum sweep."

There is a crystalline shimmer forming around our ship. That must be the shields. Doesn't look like much more than a damn soap bubble. *How about raising a friggin' mountain between us, something with some stopping power for pity's sake!*

Our squadron ships have formed a circle around us like a donut with us as the hole. I can see the barely visible shimmers of their shields. *Ok, that's a little more comforting. Not much, but a little.*

"Impact in five seconds. Four, Three, Two, One. Impact!" The universe lights up like the inside of nuclear volcano. Directly in front of the shield the missiles are exploding, painting the shield like moon sized paint gun pellets. The Triumph rocks and pitches violently. *Ok, so it's not so delicate, who knew?*

"Shields are at 90 percent. I've detected another salvo launched 30 seconds after this one, sir it should impact in 20 seconds."

"Thank you, Weaps. All hands prepare for second impact. Weaps, fire a standard missile salvo at primary target only. Fire second salvo 20 seconds later. Triumph squadron, engage enemy squadron. Try to draw their fire. Leave the primary target to Triumph."

"All squadron commanders report orders received, Captain. Impact in five seconds. Weapons reports our salvo is away." I can see little flashes of light and then the missiles leaving the Triumph and all our ships, headed towards the enemy. *Damn those things are fast!*

The second group of explosions seems to have less effect on the Triumph. We shake and juke, but nowhere near as badly. *Is that all they've got? This should be a piece of cake!*

"Shields holding at 85 percent now, sir."

"Very well, Intel, continue full scans and analysis."

"Yes sir, we're processing the squadron analysis now."

I can see the enemy ships now. They're the size of beans, twice their size the last time I saw them. *Hmmm. Gettin' kinda close aren't we?* A thought occurs to me. "PIP. Is it normal for the GHA to engage you head on?"

The AI seems to hesitate, or maybe it's just too busy to mess with me. "No, Recruit. Normally the GHA will engage in hit and run tactics in this scenario. What are you suggesting?"

"I'm not sure, PIP. Have they fired on us again?"

"Yes, two more staggered salvos have been reported, thirty seconds apart."

"Do we know yet what the target ship is?"

"We do not. Our scans do not indicate any abnormal power or weapons signatures beyond an unusually dense core."

"Core? What's a core?"

"The ships power source. It's usually placed near the center of all ships."

"How unusually dense, PIP?"

"Analysis is difficult, Mr. Jasper, as the ship has just raised an interference shield that our scanners cannot penetrate. That is also unusual for a GHA battle ship. Once in battle, there is no need for a scanner shield. Wait while I pass this information to the bridge."

Ok. What is that ship hiding and why is its core so dense? The virtual hair on the back of my virtual neck is raising. *Somethin' ain't right.* Then I notice that the ships around the target seemed to be falling back, still firing but letting the big battleship get ahead of them. *Why would you engage the Triumph, all guns blazing and then fall behind?*

Then it hits me like a bag of bad artichokes. "Trap!" I yell. "PIP, the support ships are falling back. It's a trap to lure us in close enough for something big!"

"I've analyzed your observations, Recruit, and I concur. I've notified the bridge." I swoop down to the bridge and see the Captain as she turns to the DO. "Fire broad spectrum salvo at target group NOW, Weaps. Follow in 15 seconds with another broad salvo." She turns and rapid fires more orders. "The instant the first salvo detonates turn the squadron hard to 110.231 and accelerate to maximum speed."

I can see that most of the enemy support ships have fallen behind the huge battleship, and some are even swerving away.

"First salvo will detonate in three seconds, preparing second salvo and evasive maneuver. Triumph squadron prepare for emergency turn maneuver." I can see everyone tense as the first wave of our missiles lights up the shields surrounding the enemy vessels. Then the second wave of missiles is launched like a swarm of angry hornets. I'm not prepared for this Navy's version of a 'hard to port'. Suddenly I'm being whipped around the ship on a long, invisible rope, tumbling head over heels, the stars and ships and lights spinning in crazy circles. *Can you virtually up chuck?*

PIP pipes up in my head, "Disengaging simulation, Recruit." *Oh crap!* And suddenly I'm back in the lounge on the floor, on my back waving my arms and legs wildly. Arlo is perched on my chest looking down, one little front leg raised above his pointy head.

"Relax, dude. You're embarrassing me with all that flailing around. A little dignity would be good here." With that he marches off my chest, and hops up on a chair, looking out the screen "Let's hope you were right, Dude. The Ship said the Captain was about to engage that big ass ship just before you blew the panic whistle."

The space outside the lounge screen suddenly turns brilliant neon blue and red. The ship lurches and I hear the terrifying screeches and groans of over stressed metals. I stumble to my feet as alarms start sounding, the ship continuing to ride the blast wave like a paper cup in a Texas tornado.

The searing, bright rings of the blast wash over and through the Triumph. My eyes are glued to the point where the enemy ship used to be. *Uh, oh. This is not good.* A sphere of roiling black, red and dark orange energy is expanding at an insane rate outwards. *My God, it's like we set off a super nova in our backyard.*

"All hands, emergency damage control stations. Seal off all sections and report damage to the bridge." The nightmare ball of swirling, writhing energy fills the screen completely just as I hear, "Incoming blast wave, all hands sta.." And then the big brother of the first blast strikes us, and I'm spinning in the air towards the wall. *Great, another trip to the goo pit.* I hit the wall hard and black out.

*****

G'rgnash's huge oval eyes are almost popping out of their sockets in disbelief. All four tentacle arms are splayed out fully, each with the four mini-tentacle 'fingers' vibrating wildly, whipping the clear fluid filling the control room into small whirls of foam. Patches of dark greens, blues and yellow appear, pulse and disappear all over the dark red skin of his massive, baggy head. The four 'leg' tentacles are rigidly straight, holding the Squadron Commander at his full twelve foot height.

His huge circular mouth, ringed with rows of needle-sharp fangs, stretches open and emits a screech that reverberates off the walls of the control room. The bright pink coral cave of the control room is roughly a 50 foot hemispherical dome. It has weirdly shaped seats and couches arranged at different heights all the way around, each occupied by a bizarre creature intent on the controls in front of it.

Dozens of aquatic species are frantically swimming, humping, crawling and squirting around the cavern, clicking and squawking at each other. Oddly, all the creatures seem to instinctively avoid coming anywhere near their raging Octozoid commander.

Another fierce scream makes the crew cringe further into their console couches, hoping not to draw attention to themselves as their commander vents his outrage. The thin bubbling fluid surrounding them allows them to survive while in the ship, but provides no protection from the wails of his displeasure.

G'rgnash brings a powerful arm down on his blue coral command chair, splintering a section and sending the fractured pieces of the living chair spinning off in all directions. He screams, "Sppssellzw-kkwsawallsllwexx!--fnseiilcsl!" [***Author's Note:** OK, so for those of you who skipped xenolinguistics class to make out in the parking lot, I'll translate for you. Really! How do you get by without understanding Octix or Squeezle or the other GHA forms of communication? You're welcome.*] He screams, "You missed, Spectum, damn you to Xrecxot [**a mythical waterless, volcanic* *planet used to scare the bejesus out of little squidlings*], you bloody missed! Even with the most powerful weapon the Clic'Toc guild has ever produced, you couldn't destroy the cursed Triumph! Ackckckckck." G'rgnash smashes more and more of his coral mount, pounding it with each arm to emphasize his displeasure. He turns to his second in command, standing stoically next to him.

Spectum is a Squeez; an eight foot serpent species with four long arms and four legs. Spectum's glossy black tubular body resembles a giant electric eel. His agitation is evident by the waves of brilliant green electrical arcs whizzing up and down his body. He's boiling inside, trying to keep his anger in control. *You bumbling scissax [*sphincter head]! If your cowardly escort Captains hadn't bolted just before detonation, the Triumph would be space dust right now*. Instead he straightened to his full height, and managed to get his emotions under control. The electrical display dimmed to a constant wave of dim blue waves traveling up and down his back, to signal subservience.

"A most regrettable miscalculation, Commander. However, we have proved the weapon's capabilities, and the Triumph did not escape unscarred. Our sensors show the blast destroyed several of the surface scum's ships, and the Triumph itself was badly damaged." Spectum hisses a question to a shivering creature cowering at a small CCC [***Coral Communications Console**]. The Skidix is a four foot long, bright yellow, shrimp-like creature. The poor creature's spindly arms race over the controls, and then suddenly stop. The large, yellow head is rapidly turning almost crimson as it turns back to Spectum; its antennas lower, and the huge luminescent eyes stare at the Squeez. The eyes dart left and right as it nervously chitters a response.

Spectum slowly extends a razor sharp talon to a spot between the Skidix large eyes. The Squeezs body convulses, a wave rapidly rising from the tip of his tail to his extended talon. A brilliant orange arc travels just behind his quivering flesh, growing brighter and larger, traveling all the way up his squirming body, and out the extended arm, until it jumps from the tip of his talon to the unfortunate Skidix head. The poor creature's body starts vibrating wildly, and a gaping hole appears, growing larger and larger until finally the head explodes in a pink mist, drifting outward like a hideous halo. The body shakes for a moment longer, and then slowly collapses in a heap.

Spectum kicks the smoldering shell down a hole in the floor then slowly turns back to his commander. "It seems that the Triumph, though heavily damaged, was able to return to the FTG armada. Shall we pursue her, Commander?" A fresh Skidix scrambles from another hole in the coral, taking up the vacated position on the console, its antenna are quivering uncontrollably.

Let's see your vaulted bravery now, my commander, Spectum sneers inwardly. He knows his commander will find an excuse to withdraw now that they've shown their hand to the FTG forces.

G'rgnash knows he is being tested by the Squeez, and though he's furious, he forces himself to relax and think. *I'll make you regret your impudence, you sniveling sea-snake. But not today.*

He slowly eases his body into the command chair, using the suction cups lining his arms and legs to gracefully float into the deep blue living coral. "As you said Spectum, we've performed our primary mission of testing the new weapon. Pursuing the Triumph now would be futile and a waste of time." Flipping an extended tentacle tip impatiently he continues, "Notify the squadron to reform and transit to our next rendezvous immediately."

A small Skidix skitters too close to the fuming hulk and pays the price. A red tentacle flashes out, snatching the frantic creature before it can escape. G'rgnash shoves half the squirming body into his open mouth and crunches down, biting it in half. Waving the remainder of the still quivering, pale morsel at Spectum he croaks, "We'll find another way to lure in that disgusting land vermin, Starla. I will delight in sending that bag of bones into Hell." [*Yes, it means the same thing. What are the chances?*]

*****

Just once I'd like to wake up without a Buick parked on my head.

"Jake, are going to sleep all day, or what?" Arlo's voice is echoing in my aching noggin. "You need to wake up, man, you're freaking me out."

"Hmm. Sure, Arlo, sure. Take it easy, buddy. I was having a great dream about space battles and gorgeous pink haired sailors. Gimme a second to shake off this damn headache, ok?" Opening my eyes I can see the blue and white of the ships sick bay, and the dream is real again. *Oh, my.*

The bed feels familiar but this time I'm not restrained, I can glance around. Bad idea. Instant brain explosion. Pitchforks through the eyeballs, banshees in the ears and a nice little cherry bomb explosion right there in the back. Ow!

"Please remind still, Recruit, Ship is still working on your injuries. Or do I need to restrain you?" The silky voice reminds me of warm honey and cinnamon. It's Lieutenant Tillet, my favorite pixie.

"Lieutenant, it's so good to see you again. Or not see you, I guess. Uh, to paraphrase one of my heroes; 'the ship?'" I can't help the reference to Spock, but damn it I want to know what happened. "Hello? I don't want to bother you, but if I try to turn my head it's going to fall off."

I hear her step around from behind the bed to stand between me and the consoles. *Oh my God, no!* The right side of her face is bright pink and mottled, the hair burned down to nubs. A clear gel is flowing over the wound like something alive. Her right shoulder, collar bone, and arm down to the elbow are covered in the same undulating, clear gel. Pixie sits in the chair, her eyes lock onto mine.

"It's not as bad as you might think, Mr. Jasper. As soon as a healing tank is available, I'll be able to rejuv. There's a good chance I'll keep my sight and regain use of my arm. I have you to thank for that." She tries to smile but I can see the twinge of pain. "And I intend to repay that debt tenfold if you stay with us, Jake."

She reaches out with her other hand and brushes the hair from my eyes. "But you need to relax, and let the sick bay AI finish your repairs. I don't think you'll need to use the tanks. Time to go back to sleep." She turns and starts to press something on the panel.

"Wait. Please. Tell me what happened. I don't remember anything after that sharp left turn we made; I blacked out," I say sheepishly.

She turns back to me, her voice is all business again. "The short version, Recruit, is that your analysis of the trap was seconds ahead of everyone else's, and those seconds saved the lives of thousands onboard Triumph and in our squadron. Now it's time for you to sleep." She turns to the panel and presses some more buttons. I can feel a warm, liquid sleep starting at my toes and fingers working inwards. I feel like I just chugged a triple martini with three olives. *Hmmmm.*

"Oh, now that feels nice, Miss Pixie. Umm. I'll want to hear more when I wakey, wakey, ok?" The last thing I see is her beautiful but kinda blurry pixie face bending towards me, and then she lays a warm, wet kiss on my lips. *Umm, that's pretty damn nice too.*

Chapter Ten

"This is getting old, mate." Arlo's voice brings me out of my peaceful slumber. Damn that scaly bastard; that was an excellent dream. "Shake your arse Jake; they want us on the bridge." Prying my eyes open I look around the room. We're alone except for the softly beeping consoles. *Why the hell is there always some silly blinking display on every screen? You people ever hear of a screen saver?* I decide to risk the brain flair again, sitting up slowly. Nothing happens. No pain. *Now that's more like it!*

"Ok, keep your slimy hide on, buddy, I'm getting up." There's a uniform on the chair, so I slide off the bed and pad over to get dressed. I've got to talk to them about the fancy pajamas that pass for a uniform here. "Ok, fine. I'm up. I'm dressed. All gussied up and nowhere to go, man."

Then something hits me and I turn to my little lizard 'partner'. "Hey, Arlo. Are you ok? Were you hurt little buddy?"

Arlo's voice is raspy and sarcastic. "Nice of you to remember me, 'partner'." There is a cold, reptilian pause and then, "Hey, don't worry about it, Jake. I got tossed on top of you so I had a soft landing. No harm, no foul. I'm fine."

Relief rushes over me and maybe just a little guilt. "Sorry, dude. Not your normal day, if you know what I mean." I sit back on the bed, ready to contemplate the lint in my navel. "So. If we're wanted on the bridge, how do we get there? I have no idea how to snag one of those fancy skateboards, and Lieutenant Tillet seems to be otherwise occupied." *Oops, silly me.* "PIP. Are you listening in?"

"Yes, Mr. Jasper. I've been waiting for you to contact me. Standby, I've notified Lieutenant Tillet that you are ready. She will be here in two minutes. Is there anything you need?"

Lots of things come to mind; a cold beer, hot wings, getting my sanity back. But instead I say, "Yeah, PIP. How bad was it? I know we got caught in the blast. Lieutenant Tillet put me under before she could tell me more."

"We suffered only 713 casualties and only one ship was damaged beyond repair, Mr. Jake. Considering the magnitude of the blast, we were very fortunate."

I stagger back to the chair and sit, unbelieving. "Only 713, PIP? Only? 713 souls dead, vaporized. How can you say it was 'only' 713? My God." *What kind of beings are these FTGs? Is life so cheap to them?*

"Mr. Jasper, I understand your concern, but I don't think you understand fully. Were it not for your early warning, we almost certainly would have lost most of the squadron. That's over 150,000 beings, Mr. Jasper. Now stand please, Lieutenant Tillet is arriving, and wants you ready to leave immediately."

I can barely stand. *150,000? Oh my God.* The wall morphs and Lieutenant Tillet glides into the room on a tile, hovering next to me. Her right side is now encased in some kind of skintight white substance. Her face has the same skin gel but it's clear. The skin beneath the gel is healing; even the hair is coming back in. I wonder if this is the same stuff I saw earlier, and it's changing somehow.

"Grab your partner and hop on, Mr. Jasper, we are not going to keep the Admiral waiting." She actually smiles at me without wincing, motioning to the tile.

I reach for Arlo. He hops up my arm to sit on my shoulder. His little eye rotates to fix me in weird stare. "Outstanding, partner. Time to saddle up and meet the head honcho!"

"Can it Arlo. Let's go." I turn and step up on the tile next to the Lieutenant. "We're ready, sir. I think I've made up my mind about staying." She turns to me as we start forward. "I'm afraid your decision will have to wait a little while longer, Recruit. That's not why you were summoned to the bridge. Quiet now, Jake, I need to bend a few transport rules to get you there quickly."

The tile shoots forward through the wall, and almost immediately we swerve 'up' towards the bridge. The central shaft is clogged with speeding tiles and flying boxes of all sizes. And smoke. Smoke of every color. The ship has black and red wounds over at least a quarter of her inside shaft. I can only imagine what her outer hull must look like.

We juke and weave around blasted compartment walls and massive beams sticking out at all angles into the shaft. There are cables and wires hanging from every entrance, some of them with a bright glowing blue fire shooting out of the ends. Sparks and hot metal are flowing like lava from hundreds of gaping holes in the shaft walls.

There's a muffled thump of an explosion below us. A fountain of debris is flying into the shaft from an open gash in the inner hull. A huge ragged chunk of gleaming white console flies across the shaft to the other side, smashing against a robot of some kind, sending it flying 'down', end over end, flailing its extensions like a manic rag doll.

The shaft is alive with crewmen on flying tiles of all sizes, and hosts of flying robots trying to contain and repair the damage. The image of a huge termite hill from the nature channel flashes through my mind.

Then suddenly we're there, tilting again and coming to a stop just below the bridge upper tier. Tillet doesn't even wait for the tile to stop before she jumps off. She turns to me and holds out her good hand to help me off. After guiding me to stand next to her, she turns forward again. *What the hell is going on? It's too soon for a firing squad, right?*

Tillet turns her freaky, but pretty head slightly towards me and says, "Stand at attention, if you please Mr. Jasper." She smiles and whispers softly, "Make me proud, Jake." Then her Lieutenant's stone face returns as she faces the bridge.

Lieutenant Commander Betzel is standing next to the captain's chair, her uniform immaculate. She must pour herself into it, it show every delicious curve. *How can anyone focus on their jobs here? It's like being in the Playboy Mansion during military appreciation week.* I wouldn't be surprised to see Hef, sporting a pipe and smoking jacket, leaning up against a console. *Hmm. I wonder if he's one of them.*

The Commander's stance is all business though, and it's an incredible combination of femininity and authority. Captain Starla stands from her chair, turns to Betzel. ""XO, keep me appraised of the pursuit of the GHA attack force. Notify the Admiral that I'm on my way and prepare my launch. You have the con." A brief salute and she starts towards us. Behind her the XO returns the salute and turns back to the chair, still standing to the side but putting her right hand on the back of the chair. She starts barking orders like a machine gun.

I only half hear the XO's voice as I watch Captain Starla walking towards us. Her uniform is spotless and brilliant white, gold buttons and bars everywhere. It's tailored to perfection. I can see the edge of her pant crease from here, but there's something wrong with the uniform.

She has a controlled smile on her face as she approaches and salutes Lieutenant Tillet. As she turns to the Lieutenant, I can see that the back of her head is covered in that strange, undulating white gel. It disappears down her neck and into her uniform. Now I can see that the uniform is actually flowing over that gel, all over her back and down over the curve of her ass, and down her right leg. *Someone else had a close call. Damn.*

Her voice snaps me out of my shock. "Good to see you back with us, Mr. Jasper. And you as well, Arlo." Turning to Tillet she says, "Lieutenant, bring this recruit, his partner and follow me, we don't want to keep the Admiral waiting." With that, Pixie steps on the tile, the Captain to her left, then motions for me to step to her right.

"Step lively Recruit."

I step up to Pixie's right and suddenly we're airborne, or tile-borne, or whatever. We're off like a herd of turtles.

"Make your best time to my launch bay, Lieutenant." To me she says, "Please try to be on your best behavior Mr. Jasper. You will be reflecting upon the Triumph, and the crew that serves her."

"Yes, ma'am. Of course. May I ask where we are going and why?"

"No, Mr. Jasper, you may not. Silence please. We don't want to distract the Lieutenant and end up in the tanks again." Her voice is stern, but her face has a slight smile.

Evidently there is an overdrive on these platforms, because I swear we've just got started down the shaft when Pixie turns hard to starboard and into a huge, cavernous compartment. She doesn't slow down as we shoot past row upon row of ships the size of yachts, bristling with pointy things that look deadly. There are hundreds of men, women and whatever the hell those things are, swarming around the vessels. They're dressed in silver, gray and black. It reminds me of the scenes of an aircraft carrier when flight operations are being conducted.

    We skim barely ten feet above the ships and crew. Tillet isn't slowing down, and the outer wall is coming up fast. I'm about to yell a warning when the tile takes a hard left into another bay, tucked away at the end. Slowing from a bazillion to zip in a few feet, we settle directly in front of a gleaming white and silver ship the size of an old WWII destroyer. I crane my neck to take it in. As huge as it is, there are still hundreds of feet of clearance between it and the roof of the bay.

    Arlo's tail smacks the back of my neck. "Dude, when do we get one of those? I want to take Leeta out for spin, man."

    "I don't think a lowly recruit gets his own Mega Coupe Deluxe, but I'll check it out for you, buddy." I had to agree with Arlo, I want one of those. Damn, that's a beautiful ship!

    "Recruit! Shake a leg or I'll leave you behind!" The Captain and Tillet are half way up the silver ramp. *Oops.*

    I start off at a trot to catch up; I can feel Arlo's little claws digging into the shoulder pad. "Yes, sir." Running up the ramp. I can feel it retracting into the side of the ship. *Really? What's the damn hurry? This is no way to treat someone you want to join the space patrol is it?* I barely make it into the hatch before it morphs into a wall. Arlo is miffed at me from the sound of his little voice. "That was close, Rube, stop gawking and pay attention!"

    The inside of the launch is more polished white and silver. Red uniformed marines stand at attention on either side of the corridor as our party passes. The crew is scrambling everywhere; men, women and again, just what the hell are those? I pick up the pace to stay close to the Captain. Tillet steps back to flank me.

"Keep up, Mr. Jasper. We'll be seated behind the Captain. Please hold your questions a bit longer. We'll be on the flag ship in a few minutes." She guides me to the bridge section, where the Captain is standing next to the pilot's chair, looking out the forward screens. Pixie moves us to a seat behind the pilot.

Captain Starla taps the shoulder of one of those 'what the hell?' beings in the pilot's chair and says, "Lift as soon and possible, Mr. Cihcta, I want best speed to the flag ship."

The pilots face is as gray and square as one of those toy rockem' sockem' robots. His voice sounds like rocks being crushed between steel drums. "Magnetic moorings have retracted, sir, we are underway." His hands are massive, but seem to fly over the console in front of him. "ETA to Brilliant is 1.6 minutes."

I can see through the screen that we've lifted, and are pivoting towards the bay opening. He's flipping us around like a Frisbee, then suddenly we shoot forward and we're outside the Triumph, into open space. At first all I can see is the speckled black void. Then the curve of Triumph comes into view as the pilot maneuvers our ship around.

We've got to be miles away from Triumph by now, yet its size is staggering. I can't get a reference that my mind will accept, but I swear the aircraft carrier USS Enterprise would look like a rubber ducky next to this behemoth. We pick up speed as we whip around the ship. Our destination must be on the other side.

"Beautiful, isn't she, Mr. Jasper?" says Tillet in a low voice. "Triumph is a Nova class battleship of the line, out of the Nubus yards for about three standard cycles now. We're very proud of her, and of her crew." There is genuine pride in her smooth voice. I know that feeling of pride. I'm surprised to realize just how much I've missed it. Excellence breeds excellence.

As we continue to zip around the ship my gut suddenly tightens into a dark knot. I barely get a chance to take in the swath of destruction on the ship before we're past it, and speeding out into space. Playing back the quick look in my mind, I can see the giant black and red wound that covers a full quarter of the upper hull, stopping just below the bridge section. Thousands of tiny figures and what must be repair robotics are swirling around the gaping hole in a mad dance. Green and blue fumes and sparks were flaring everywhere. Oh my God, the explosion got through the shields and took a bite out of Triumph.

I glance at Tillet's wounds and wonder where she was during the blast, and how she ever survived that. She seems to sense my shock, reaching over to touch my hand briefly before returning it to her lap. That brief touch was more than a comforting pat. Her brief look was full of sorrow and something else. "It could have been much, much worse, Jake," she says softly. Then she turns back to the screen.

The launch is weaving around ships of all sizes, some spewing multicolored vapors and debris far worse than Triumph. Our destination slowly comes into view. At first it looks like another Nova class ship, like Triumph. No, I can see now that it's top and bottom tori sections are much larger than Triumphs. As we speed towards it, I realize how much bigger. *Damn, that ship has to be five times the size of Triumph!* As I lean in to ask Tillet about the ship, the pilot speaks.

"FTG Brilliant, this is Triumph Prime. Requesting immediate docking," his voice has a shocking command quality for a load of wet gravel.

I hear the response over the launch's intercom. "FTG Triumph, this is Brilliant. Permission granted. Please follow beacons into the Admirals bay. Brilliant Prime extends his greetings to all aboard. You are expected on the bridge."

I sense Captain Starla's ramrod back stiffen even more somehow. There is a very slight smile on her luscious lips as she gives Tillet and me a slight nod, and then faces forward again.

Without looking back at us she says, "Lieutenant Tillet, please instruct your recruit as to proper protocol for meeting the Admiral. This will be short and sweet, and I don't want him to tell the Admiral anything about switches or valves. For now anyway." I can see the smile broaden, and then I realize she's heard about my conversation with the Chief Engineer. *Oops.*

I take a chance and say, "I'll be a proper and poised white hat, sir. I wouldn't embarrass the Triumph for my life. I have the deepest respect for authority you know." Now it was my turn to smile. I look to my right, and see Tillet's smile is ear to ear. She looks like she's going to bust a gusset trying not to laugh out loud.

Pixie composes herself and says, "Aye, aye Captain. I'll make sure Mr. Jasper is straight and squared away." I get another brief pat on the hand, this time with a little squeeze that makes the Private's privates come to attention.

The launch makes a last second swerve to the right and enters a huge bay. If that's the Admiral's launch, there is a serious gold shortage somewhere. The ship we're landing next to is three times the size of ours, and seems to glow as if alive. It's shot through with gold, silver and eye numbing ebony streaks along its hot, white frame.

We land without a bump in an open slot next to it. Captain Starla turns and faces us as we rise. "Let's get this over with Lieutenant. I have a ship to make ready." She turns to me and says, "And you have a decision to make soon recruit." As she walks past us Tillet nudges me to step in behind.

Walking down the launch ramp is like stepping into Oz. There is an honor guard of ten huge, red uniformed Marines standing at attention. As Captain Starla steps off the ramp onto the deck, the first one in line salutes and barks crisply, "Welcome aboard, Triumph. The Admiral is on the bridge. Please follow me." When Captain Starla returns his salute, he turns and walks through the line. We follow close behind. *Even the damn Marines are bigger on this ship!*

The Captain of the Guard steps up on a large golden tile motioning for us to follow. No sooner have we all stepped up than it starts to speed through the ship. It's like being inside Dallas, surround by a funky bubble. We ride in silence, me gawking like a hick from the sticks, taking in this fantastic dream city. There are ships bigger than the Triumph's launch whizzing by, and thousands of smaller vessels everywhere. It's like watching one of those time lapse movies of down town New York City or LA streets, except nobody stops for any lights.

"Holy crap, Partner! We're going to need a GPS just to find our way back from the friggin' bathroom in this place!" Arlo's eyes are spinning like tiny gyroscopes gone wild. "Don't you dare lose track of Ms. Pixie, or we could starve before we find a McDonalds." His left eye snaps to focus on me. "By the way, I'm hungry and I gotta go soon."

Suddenly we shoot past a squad of marines on red tiles. They're hell bent for faux leather somewhere else, disappearing into the central shaft. I get a brief view of the shaft before we turn 'up' with our heads turned inwards. *Jesus! The shaft could probably hold the Triumph!* I must have let out an eek or something, because I feel Tillet's hand squeeze mine. She motions with her other hand towards her open mouth, closes it and then raises her eyebrows to me. *Oh! Right!* I shut my gaping mouth. I can feel the red rush up my face. *Well hell, once a rube always a rube.* It's damn overwhelming is my only defense.

Seconds later we're at the bridge section. We make a sharp twist and 90 degree tilt out of the shaft and into the massive control section. The tile settles on the deck just below the command chair and control panels. We step off the tile and a marine motions us to one side to wait.

A tall commanding looking officer in white and gold stands up from the central command chair. He turns to an officer on his right, an eight foot humanoid with three large red eyes. "Mr. Pashta, gather the fleet. Let me know when we're ready to leave station. You have the bridge." The huge whatever it is salutes back and I heard Goldie Hawn's voice respond, "I relieve you sir." It takes everything I have not to giggle. "Helm, notify the fleet to prepare to leave station." Goldie, I mean big foot turns to his post standing next to the chair.

The Admiral scans our party as he descends the tiers to our level. His left hand is behind his back, his right holds some kind of staff. His face is stern and tight. I'm looking for extra parts like eyes and horns, but damn if he doesn't look human.

Captain Starla snaps a salute. "FTG Triumph at your service, sir." She waits for the returned salute. Admiral Izzac is taking his time, looking me over from top to bottom. Finally he returns the salute, looking stern and pissed. Then a smile breaks the tension. "Well done, Starla. I feared I had lost the valiant Triumph during that blast. Damn, we've never seen a detonation of that magnitude from the enemy. How did you know it was a trap?"

"The bridge had just noticed something strange about the enemy formation when our AI recommended evasive action. I ordered the torp spread to hide our turning. It turns out that a new recruit had seen the trap before I did." She turns to me. "May I present Recruit Jake Jasper, from Earth."

Say what? I'm too stunned to move; this is not what I was expecting.

The Admiral looks at me expectantly. Finally I manage to salute and say, "Sir. All I did was tell PIP that the support ships were peeling off instead of flying support for that big hunk of rock."

"PIP? And who is PIP, Recruit?"

"Sorry sir. It's my name for the Triumph's AI. It did say to give it a proper name so I did."

"I see. An interesting choice, most recruits just call it 'Ship'. But then you're human aren't you?" He raises his eyebrows and then smiles. "The people of Earth would be proud of you if they only knew."

The smile disappears. "Regardless, Mr. Jasper, the seconds you provided saved the lives of thousands, and I'm damn glad you spoke out. I understand you were forced to join us before you had a chance to complete your tour of Triumph, and make your recruiting decision. Is that correct?"

"Yes, sir."

"I see." He turns to Captain Starla and says, "The advanced warning was resourceful to say the least, Captain, but your torpedo mask was brilliant. I'm convinced that the cover salvo fooled the enemy into thinking you were close enough to be destroyed. My complements to Triumph, Captain, she served the fleet above and beyond today."

He turns back to me and says, "As for you, Recruit. Well done. But it's time for you to make your decision. I need Triumph as soon as possible back with the fleet. I know it's a hard choice you have to make, to leave your home and your loved ones. But everyone in this fleet has had to make the same decision."

He seems to hesitate and then says to Starla, "I'd like a moment with Mr. Jasper, if you don't mind, Captain."

Starla responds immediately, "Of course, sir, I'll contact Triumph to get an update while we wait for Recruit Jasper. By your leave, sir." She salutes the Admiral, and then starts back to the tile, Tillet at her side, already talking into her comtat.

The Admiral turns back to the front screens, but I hear through my implant, "This is terrible form, Mr. Jasper, using our link with the ship without asking you first, but I wanted you to know something, and I want to speak private. Please walk with me."

He starts forward, towards the huge screens, to a spot in front of the command chair. I automatically match his stride, coming to a halt under the immense dome overhead. I follow his gaze to the dozens of ships maneuvering into formation around Brilliant. The Admiral sighs. "This conversation needs to remain between us, Mr. Jasper, for reasons too complicated to discuss now. Can I count on you to keep it private?"

I have to concentrate a bit to speak through the implant. "Yes, sir. You can trust me, sir."

He looks directly at me for a moment, and then nods.

"I believe I can. Very well, then, here it is. I'm from Earth, Mr. Jasper, specifically Boulder, Colorado." He glances at me again and smiles. "It's important for you to know that there are other's like you in service to the FTG. Other humans, who have given their life in service, some their very lives, to protect not only Earth, but many other civilizations."

I had been wondering about that. It feels good to know I'm not the alien here. I'm getting the hang of 'thinking' my response. "Do you miss Earth, sir? Did you make the right decision?"

He shakes his head and smiles. "Direct and blunt. I could use more of that attitude here, Mr. Jasper. Yes, I miss Earth every day.

But I can tell you I've never regretted my decision to join the FTG, and protect my home world."

He seems to hesitate, and then come to a decision. "I don't often think about my past, Mr. Jasper. But seeing you reminded me of home and what I left behind." He adjusts his immaculate jacket and continues, staring ahead. "I left Earth in 1899, not long after the University opened. What a beautiful campus CU was; we were so proud. I understand it's grown a bit, is that true?"

"Quite a bit, I believe sir. Boulder is the gem of Colorado now. You said you left something behind. I take it you don't mean just your life."

"No, Mr. Jasper, I do not." By the look in his eyes I can sense what's coming, but I keep my silence. He reaches into a jacket pocket, and pulls out a small picture. He stares at the faded photograph, and gently hands it to me. "Please be careful with this Mr. Jasper, it's over a hundred years old. Everyone thinks I'm crazy for not having it laminated or converted to an image I can upload to Ship so that I can view it anytime I want. But I prefer it as it is; it seems more real that way."

I take the small, well worn picture carefully. It's the Admiral in 19th century waist coat and bowler. Next to him stands a lady dressed in a high collared, full length dress with broad hat and a small parasol. They are standing in front of the Chautauqua park dining hall in the west Boulder foothills. I can barely make out the pine covered mountains and steeply slanted flatiron rock formations above it. "She's beautiful, sir. I've been to that park; it's a wonderfully peaceful place." Handing the picture back to him, I'm suddenly moved with the reality of what he must have gone through.

His voice in my head is soft and hollow. "Her name was Sheila. We were engaged. It was supposed to be a short summer vacation for me. I was a fleet commander in the Navy at the time. Then Starla showed up to recruit me. When she showed me what the GHA was doing, I knew I had no real choice." Closing his eyes, he sighs, his shoulders seem to sag a bit. "I had to leave her, Mr. Jasper. Forever." I can see in his face that he's back there now; walking along some favorite path, arm in arm with his long lost love.

He seems to shake off his funk and turns to me, his face stern and determined. "And I'd do it again. I'm keeping Earth safe, at least for awhile. I hope you'll consider joining us, son."

There's a soft tone as the connection is broken. The Admiral motions for me to follow him back to Captain Starla and Pixie.

They exchange salutes. "Captain, return to Triumph, and prepare to get underway. Your recruit will have to make his decision on your return trip. I cannot hold the fleet any longer. Understood?"

"As you wish, Admiral. Thank you, sir." Captain Starla salutes, and turns towards the waiting tile. "This way, Mr. Jasper." Our party steps onto the tile, and we're off before I have a chance to say anything.

So, it's crunch time. I have a few minutes to decide if I want to be a rag hat again or live my retirement in peace in Port A, drinking beer and ogling the beach bunnies.

I look at Arlo sitting patiently on my shoulder. "What do you say Arlo? You're my partner here, so it's your choice too. Are you happier here than you were on Earth? Do you want to go home?" I wait for Arlo to speak up in my head as we shoot through the ship back to the launch.

He finally snaps an eye at me and says, "Hells bells no, Bucko! Let see if I have this right, partner. There's a bunch of slimy, soggy bastards who want to exterminate us, then squat on our world. We have a chance to kick their asses all the way back to Water World, and you get to wear cool pajamas. What's to choose? Let's ride, cowboy!"

Tillet leans into me and says, "I hope that smile means you've decided to stay, Jake." Her eyes were hopeful and so deep I almost fall into them. She reaches for my hand, gives it a soft squeeze, and then releases it. Then concern clouds her sweet, fairy face. "But you need to think seriously about it. There is no going back if you join. You cannot resign from service."

Captain Starla speaks without turning to us, "Lieutenant, you'll have just over two minutes to instruct Mr. Jasper on the recruitment protocol while the launch transits back to Triumph. That's all I can spare. If he decides to leave us you will take a fighter, return him to

Earth and then catch up with us." Too soon, we are back in the launch bay, making our way up the ramp.

"Yes, sir. Come sit here, Jake." Tippet takes my elbow as we enter the cockpit. She pulls me to the side, away from the pilot and Captain. The launch is away without delay, whizzing out into space.

Pixie takes my hand. "Jake, Arlo, we can talk now, I've turned off all comm links and in this area no one will hear us. The protocol the Captain mentioned is simple. Once you decide, one way or the other, you have to link with the ship AI. The AI will ask you if you want to enlist. If you say 'No' I'll take you home, no questions asked. We have agents that will help you establish a new identity, since your physical appearance is somewhat different. And we'll provide you with funds to last the rest of your life. With the rejuvs you've received you could live in very good health for at least another fifty years."

Her face is controlled as she continues, "You will never be contacted again, Jake." She seems to catch her breath before she continues. "If you answer 'Yes', the AI will ask you several questions to make sure you understand what you're getting into. Then it will ask again. That's when you must answer 'Yes' or 'No' a final time. I'm sorry you didn't get a more formal tour, but considering what you did see, I'd say you experienced more than most recruits. That's it. Do you have any questions before you contact the Ship?"

"Yeah. What about my family? What do I tell them if I decide to join? We may not be close but they'll worry if I just disappear. I don't want that on my conscience."

"Of course not, Jake." She frowns slightly and says, "Would they believe that you want to take a year and tour the world, travel to all the places you've always dreamed of seeing? Many recruits do this, and then send communications whenever they can. Our agents on Earth can take care of your home and other affairs while you're away."

"Yeah, I guess that would work fine."

My head is spinning with more questions, but in my heart I know I've already made up my mind. Arlo is still perched on my shoulder eyeballing me again. "What do you think, buddy?" Arlo's eye rotates a couple of times.

"Who are you kidding, Jake? I know what you're thinking, remember? You can't tune me out and hell yes we're staying!" His little tail snaps my neck and he says, "Quit wasting time, man, we're almost back at the damn ship. Let's do this."

I can't keep the smile off my face. I face Lieutenant Pixie and say, "Arlo and I are ready to talk to the Ship now, Lieutenant."

There's hope in her eyes and a smile that melts my spine. "I'll step away, Jake and let you talk out loud. Regardless of your decision, Jake, you're an amazing man." She looks around and then rises, leans forward quickly to plants a quick kiss on my lips. The electric jolt runs from my lips down my body and snaps my toes out like spikes. Before I can react she turns and walks to the other side of the cabin without looking back. *Holy crap! That's cheating lady. But damn, if you're going to cheat, do it like that!*

"Hey, lover boy. Hey, Jake, snap out of it, man. I don't want to lose our chance at fame and glory, man, get the AI on the phone. Now!" Arlo's rant brings me back from my randy daydreams. Damn it.

I frown at Arlo and say out loud, "PIP. We'd like to enlist."

PIP sounds small and soft in the air next to my ear. "Very well, Mr. Jasper. Please consider these questions before answering. I'm monitoring you and can tell if you're lying, sir. Do you understand?"

"Yes."

"Do you understand that you may never be able to return to Earth?"

"Yes."

"Do you understand you are being recruited into the Federation of Thirteen Galaxies as an ABS; an Able Bodied Spaceman recruit, the lowest ranking in the service?"

"Yes."

"Do you understand that you're putting yourself if physical danger…"

I just have to interrupt the interview here, silly me. "PIP, I just rode out the friggin' 'Shoot out at the Space Corral' outside the ship, whipping around at friggin' warp twenty. I think I know about the friggin' danger."

"Sir, please respond as friggin' 'Yes' or friggin' 'No'."

I start laughing and can't stop. I double over and almost fall off my seat before I remember how serious this is supposed to be. "I'm sorry, PIP. Yes. Yes, I understand the danger."

"Very well. This is the last question, sir. Do you swear by your honor and personal faith that you will strive to uphold the highest standards of the Federation of Thirteen Galaxies?"

Whoa. What PIP is asking me is to accept a set of morals and military honor. But I haven't had time to live with these people yet, how can I say yes without knowing more about them? "PIP, I can't answer that question. Not unless I can ask a question first."

"I'm sorry, Mr. Jasper, but that is not part of the protocol. You must answer yes or no."

My heart sinks. "I understand PIP. But unless I know the hearts of the people I'm going to be serving with, I can't give my own heart in their service. I'm sorry. I can't do that."

I feel drained. Tillet walks over, and sits next to me. Here comes the 'I'm sorry, you failed the interview, Recruit, time to go home.' speech. "Congratulations, Jake. The AI has accepted your answers, and is ready to ask you again if you want to enlist."

"What? I don't understand. I told PIP that I couldn't enlist unless I understood more about these people, and what honor means to them. I did not say yes."

Pixie's smile is genuine and somehow relieved. "I know, Jake. That is the only response we will accept from a recruit. If you had said yes, we would have rejected you, and returned you to Earth. I can tell you now that we had to lie to you about enlistment."

My head is hurting again. I'm not great with lies. Don't like them one little bit. Lies make life hard and burn you up inside. "Lied about what part, Lieutenant?"

"If you decide to enlist, Mr. Jasper, you will serve a one cycle training period. That's about a year of Earth time. During that time you will not be allowed to return to Earth, but will undergo full training. We'll find the right rating for your talents and abilities. The

Navy and you will find out if you've got what it takes. At the end of the cycle, you can choose to leave the service. No questions will be asked, there will be no coercion to stay." She touches me on the arm again and smiles. "If you test well, the AI will ask you again. At that time, your decision will be permanent."

Crap and super crap. This changes everything. I get a chance to really know the members of the Federation and see if this is the right choice for me. It's still a big gamble. They could be lying to me again.

"No, Mr. Jasper. We are not lying to you now." PIP's voice was adamant. "We regret the necessity of the deception, sir, but we want and need recruits who can think for themselves, and make hard choices. We don't need or want followers. I hope you will forgive the lie."

I put my hand on Pixies and say, "You guys are smarter than the average bear, that's for sure." I know my answer now. "PIP, we wish to enlist." Tillet's face is beaming. She squeezes my hand and then releases it.

PIP asks again, "Very well, Mr. Jasper. This is the last question then. Jake Jasper, do you and your partner, Arlo, wish to enlist in the Space Navy of the Federation of Thirteen Galaxies?"

"Friggin' yes, PIP. Friggin' yes!"

Chapter Eleven

"Prepare to get underway, XO. Please advise the Admiral that Triumph is at his command," says Captain Starla from her chair on the bridge. Standing with Lieutenant Tillet next to the navigation station, I'm getting my first look at the fleet in transit. My heart is racing.

The XO turns to Captain Starla, with a huge smile on her face. She says, "The Brilliant extends its gratitude to Triumph prime, and to its newest recruits." She winks at me, and turns back facing forward. "All hands. Prepare to transit!"

I'm not sure what impresses me more, the sight of the star filled space morphing and folding around us, or the pinch on the ass I just got from Pixie. *Hang on, Arlo! This is going to be fun!*

The End

Want more of Arlo and Jake?

Here's a teaser of their next adventure with Pixie, Starla and the crew of the FTG Triumph!

Arlo and Jake Galactic Boot Camp

Book Two of the adventures of Arlo and Jake

Chapter One

The sleek orange and black space ship is juking back and forth, trying to evade our pursuit. I concentrate on the port particle beam cannon, and mentally command, "Fire!" A brilliant sparkling red-blue beam instantly leaps from below and left of my heads up display, reaching out to the fleeing ship. It passes harmlessly above the ship by a country mile. I look at my HUD, my Heads-Up Display readout. Ok, more precisely I missed by 800 kilometers. *Damn.* "Arlo, can you get that cannon gimbal tightened up? I'm having trouble with lateral targeting."

Arlo's voice comes through the interface, though I can't see him. "I'm on it, cowboy. Gimme a second."

The ship is starting to pull away. "Any time now, Arlo, I'm losing him."

"Got it, Jake! Nail the bastards!"

I get off two more shots in rapid succession, but both miss, though I am getting closer. Any moment they're going to fold space and I'll lose them. *That's it I'm done messing around here.* I concentrate on my weapons display, and crank up the cannon's power to twenty percent of full. I try to concentrate on the wildly gyrating ship. The green targeting brackets jerk and twist around the ship as I try to frame it inside the brackets. Finally I get a good bead, the brackets start flashing red and the gotcha tone sounds in my head. Grinning maniacally I yell, "Fire!"

Instantly a beam that's almost as big as the retreating ship erupts from below me, nailing the ship in the ass. The explosion lights up space in front of me like a galactic fireworks stand. The heated ball of molten metal becomes a rapidly expanding sphere of space goop, with more and more explosions going off, getting bigger and bigger. *Uh oh, this is not good.* I'm about to yell for evasion maneuvers when the biggest explosion yet rips through the blinding white ball of death and crashes into me. *Damn, that's gonna hurt.*

I peer through the HUD and suddenly space in front of me is clear again. The ship is hanging motionlessly just ahead of me like a frozen movie frame. *Oops, screwed the pooch again.* I wait for PIP to slap my virtual hand.

"One more time, Recruit Jasper, and this time let's try not to vaporize our ship along with the enemy, shall we?" PIP's slightly sarcastic voice sounds through my mental interface. Her voice is calm, steady with just a bit of exasperation. Exactly what you expect from an HIPP-52 Artificial Intelligence,

"Call up your engineering specs for this ship, and find the location of the power nodes. Then focus the diameter of your particle beam to 10 centimeters. Target the nodes on the enemy's starboard maneuvering nacelles. You want to disable the ship, not reduce it to star dust. Try again."

I'm sweating like a pig even though I know my body is resting comfortably in my battle couch. My mind is linked into the Battle Sim through my command link with PIP, the ship's AI. PIP is feeding me all the data for the battle simulation. These training simulations are helping Arlo and me to accept the data feed and translate it into our minds as reality.

Right now that reality is a little overwhelming. I'm floating about 100 feet 'above' the Triumph, a Nova class battle cruiser in the FTG, the Federal of Thirteen Galaxies. Actually it was thirteen but they lost one so now it's only twelve Galaxies. But they can't afford to change all the stationery so nobody says anything. My target is about one tenth as large as Triumph, and trying to evade our pursuit. My task is to stop the runaway ship without destroying it. I thought it would be an easy run. I was wrong. So far I've vaporized it three times. Not good.

"I'm having trouble calling up the specs, and handling the weapons targeting system quickly, PIP, give me a break. I've only been at this session for half an hour or so." I'm a little peeved at myself for not nailing this sim more quickly. *Why can't I concentrate today?*

"You've been running this sim for four hours, Mr. Jasper. And your lack of concentration is partially due to fatigue. I've also noticed that when you are separated from Lieutenant Tillet for more than two days, you become restless. Could that be affecting your performance?"

"PIP's right Jake, you're all over the place. You thinking about Pixie's pretty little derriere in a pink thong, aren't you?" Arlo's Scottish drawl makes him sound like Connery sometimes. "She's only been gone for a few days, can't you man up a little? Wuss."

"If I knew where your ugly little butt was, little buddy, I'd swat it. I'm not pining for Asa, and it's been 8 days I'll have you know!" I knew as soon as I said it he was right. I missed Asa a lot and it was affecting my training. "Besides, she and the Captain are due back tomorrow, right PIP?"

"That's correct, Mr. Jasper. Lieutenant Tillet contacted Triumph two hours ago. They are due back at 0700. Shall we save the simulation here, and continue tomorrow after you've had a chance to relieve your tension? Perhaps then you can again focus on your training."

I'll never get used to the casual way this culture, and its AI's talk about relationships. It's like the free love era of the 60's, only these people add responsibilities to the mix. The basic rule is to do what feels right as long as you're not hurting anyone, including yourself. And the punishment for hurting someone is severe, very severe.

"Ok, I give. Let's bag this one for now, PIP. Disconnect from sim please." My vision pops from my aerial position above the Triumph to the dim ceiling lights of the training room. At this time of cycle, I'm the only occupant of the dozen couches arranged around the small circular room. I rub my eyes and sit up. The feet of the big couches are arranged towards the center of the circle. The heads of the couches are embedded into the smooth consoles ringing the room.

Looking back at the console at the head of my couch, I can see it powering down; the smooth, lined panels dimming to dark. The foot of my couch lowers, allowing me to step out onto the smooth white floor.

On my left I can see Arlo sitting on my console, his left eye rotating around in crazy circles, his right eye fixed on me. "Wakey,

wakey, Mr. Flakey. Shake it off, Jake, I'm hungry." Arlo morphs his chameleon skin and almost disappears into the console background. *Show off.*

Arlo morphs back to his normal mottled green. His gravelly voice pipes up in my head, "Come on, buddy, I need some grubs and you need that junk you eat and a beer."

Arlo and I have a telepathic link that doesn't depend on my comm implant. Of course the fact that Arlo, who used to be my pet lizard, is now my intellectual equal and 'partner' in the FTG Navy still stops me in my tracks sometimes.

PIP's voice sounds from the room intercom, "I believe Arlo is correct, Mr. Jasper. You've exceeded your allotted time in the sim once again. You need to eat and then rest. I have a transport tile waiting outside. It will take you to the closest crews lounge."

I walk over and reach out my arm for Arlo. He ambles up to his normal perch on my shoulder, his eye zeroing in on me. "Let's boogie, Bronco Billy, you've nuked enough bad guys for today." With that he settles down on my shoulder and starts that weird jerky, rotating eye trick. I can't watch it for more than a few seconds. Sheesh, that's just creepy.

A door morphs behind my couch and I see the small red tile floating just an inch off the deck. I step up and feel the field grab my body firmly. Without a pause it rises a few more inches and starts zipping through corridors, barely avoiding all the other tiles zipping around. I don't have to concentrate on the tile this time because PIP is guiding it, so I just sit back, er, stand back, and enjoy the ride.

We race through the corridors towards the central access shaft of the immense war ship, passing members of hundreds of different races, and bots of all shapes and sizes. I'm still not used to the diversity of species that crew the Triumph. Each crewman is here because their home world has been or will be threatened with extinction. Like me and Arlo, each has agreed to serve in the Space Navy of the FTG, the only force that stands in the way of the GHA, the Galactic Houses of Aquinoxous.

I'm still learning about the struggle, the FTG and GHA through the training and holo studies programs. I've been soaking up these studies into the holo room, witnessing the long histories of both sides. Sometimes PIP can feed me the data directly into my implant so that I get a 'burst' of information. Other times, I lay on the training couch and PIP takes Arlo and me through some history or protocol lesson. These are harder for us, but it's still better than anything I experienced in school or military training. Imagine being able to sit on a park bench under the trees on some university campus and talk to a famous philosopher or scientist or inventor. I mean really talk to them, just like they were there with you.

I think I've stretched the intent of my lessons a few times but PIP and Asa have tolerated my requests most of the time.

I've discussed revolution and freedom with Ben Franklin. Francis Bacon taught me the basics of Empiricism. I've learned art, invention and engineering with Leonardo Da Vinci (what an ego!). And I've learned many new subjects with beings that I didn't even know existed.

The tile is picking up speed again and we swoosh out into the central shaft. PIP twists the tile and points us 'down', away from the Bridge section. "Stop showing off, PIP, my stomach still has problems with these little roller coaster rides!"

"As you wish, Mr. Jasper," PIP says in my head. The tile slows to sub-upchuck speed. "We're three minutes from Crews Lounge twenty two."

"How many friggin' drinkin' holes do we have on this flying stack of donuts?" Arlo's voice was a teensy bit tight. I can tell he's not having a lot of fun gyrating around the ship either. "Can we just find one and set this souped up Frisbee on the ground? I'm hungry!"

"There are over 500 crews' lounges on the Triumph, Arlo. I'm taking you to the closest that can service your species."

"Fine. Can you get us to twenty-two without scaring the crap out of us? Jake isn't much of a partner when he's hysterical," whines Arlo.

"OK, that's enough Arlo. And I was not hysterical yesterday. That was an excited exuberance. I was absolutely exuberant that we almost splattered like Wiley Coyote against that bulkhead. Excited, yeah that's just how I roll." *OK, fine. I was screaming like a liberal Democrat at an NRA convention. So what?*

Follow the adventures of Arlo and Jake as they try to stay alive long enough to graduate from space cadet boot camp in:

'Arlo and Jake'
'Galactic Boot Camp'

About the Author

Gary Alan Henson served for 9 years in the US Naval Nuclear Submarine service. He has also served a lifetime as a proud father, grandfather and husband.

He was a Machinist Mate, a Lab Technician, an air compressor mechanic, a computer tape drive technician and a test computer technician. Then he shifted to software in the 80s and never looked back.

Gary and his wife live in beautiful north Texas, just close enough to first spoil and then return their granddaughters.

Made in the USA
Columbia, SC
08 September 2018